D0628423

To Sam, all my best — Jim

The
Watchmaker's
Son

James T. Vance

Published by FastPencil Publishing

James T. Vance

The Watchmaker's Son

First Edition

Print edition ISBN: 9781495831003

http://www.fastpencil.com

Printed in the United States of America

Table of Contents

Dedication vii

1 Over and Back Again 9

2 More Than One 13

3 News: Good or Bad 21

4 Looking for a Home 29

5 The Sins Of Society 33

6 Sunday Dinner 37

7 The Watchmaker's Son 45

8 DeSeco Family Reunion 51

9 The Psychiatrist 57

10 Doctor Fitzgibbons 67

11 A Mellow Time 75

12 Murder in King Of Prussia 85

13 Decetive Sullivan 91

14 Old Friends Are the Best Friends 97

15 Uncle Carlo 105

16 Monsignor Avandonto 113

17 Sergeant Baker 123

18 Uptight 129

19 More Information 139

20 Last Stand..149

21 The Way It Is 153

22 Time to Reflect..161

Epilogue Faith, Love, Family, Time......................................165

Acknowledgments 171

About the author..173

To my wife Diane for her love and encouragement. To my brothers Pat and Nick for their senses of humor. To all my aunts, uncles, and cousins, the Serafinos from my mother's family, and the Avanzatos (Vances) from my father's family. We had fun times growing up together, and it continues on into adulthood. To Diane's family. We enjoy spending time together. To all my very dear friends for all the laughter and happy times we continue to have and share. To all the families from every nationality. Believe in faith, love of family, and laughter with all friends.

❧

1 Over and Back Again

D etective Anthony Lupo was back on the murder case again, the same case that involved the death of five people, the case that embroiled a town in controversy, conflict, and fear for almost six years from 1961 to 1966 all because of an Italian superstition that certain families believed is some type of evil curse. The murder case also involved money, money that was not paid to certain individuals for a particular service that was rendered. There was the possibility of money laundering and loan sharking. It was a murder case that involved love, family, money, and fear. Detective Anthony Lupo only wanted to know two things about the murders of five business people. Who really committed the murders and why?

These murders may have had their start back in the early1950's and continued up to the death of five people during the early1960's into the middle of 1966. In the town of North Oak, Pennsylvania that lies about 20 miles just outside of Philadelphia, some people were very afraid of a superstition created by a certain person or some very strange people.They also were terrified that this type of power and belief could actually make you sick or hurt you in some mysterious way. It is the look, the way their eyes stare at you. It is a spell that can upset you. It is called the Malocchio or Fatura. In English it would be called the Evil Eye, the OverLooks, or the Black Hand. It is true that some would call them witches and warlocks. Quite a few people in that town were very afraid of that kind of person or the people who got themselves involved with individuals that promoted this type of belief. It was concentrated in the Italian section of town. Some people understood this type of voodoo or superstition or whatever you want to call it because of their Italian heritage. Other Italian people, who did not understand or believe in it, would question the people who did believe in this curse. They questioned if they would ever understand what people can do with some of the power they feel that they possess or the fear they can put in someone. This power is very questionable, but in some cases the fear is real. It can scare the hell out of you or maybe put some hell into you. Should people care about the superstition and maybe try and understand this fear? This type of superstition and fear caused a businessman, a local jeweler who was a watchmaker, to lose almost $10,000. It was a very unusual circumstance that made local news and was reported in the local newspaper in North Oak, as the "Evil Eye Case." It was definitely something to be concerned about. In the early 1950's someone could buy a house for $10,000. It also could be a year's salary for the working middle-class person. Ten thousand dollars was a good bit of money.

Some people question the superstition and the fear. Many did not question the fear, but they tried to understand it, simply because someone needed to catch the killer or killers. A police detective was trying to solve this murder case that started in early 1961 and followed through to 1966 when a suspect was arrested for the "Evil Eye Murder Case". It may have involved other aspects besides evil and fear, aspects such as money. Some people believe that money is the root of all evil, and this was the murder of some local business people who not only believed in the superstitious curse but were people who were in the business of lending money to certain families and people who were involved in business that the police called money laundering or loan sharking. This murder case took a whole different understanding. The North Oak Police Department thought it was over, the end of all the killings and the crazy belief of the curse, but it was not over.

Some people from good, healthy, and caring families believed in some crazy superstitions. They believed that some one could give a person the evil eye by an Italian hand-gesture that is formed with a fist by extending the index and little finger while holding the middle finger and ring finger down with the thumb. This type of gesture is called the "devil's horns." Now there were also people who believed that a person could not receive the Malocchio (evil eye) by wearing certain charms or medallions around his neck. Some Italians would wear a horn (*cornetto*) that resembles a chili pepper. This is to ward off any type of evil that may come their way. Back in the day some remember when they were young if one of their family members would get a headache or fill sick, they would call on one of their older relatives who is familiar with that type of belief and who was capable of relieving an individual from this superstitious curse. They would tell the older relative that they needed help because someone put the overlooks on them. The overlooks was another form of saying the Malocchio or evil eye.

People remember the Evil Eye Murder case and remember some of the bad and sad things that happened in and around their hometown. Others remember the good times, good people, and good things that happened growing up. There was a lot of good in and around their hometown, and there were a lot of good people from various nationalities. The most important part of their life growing up as an Italian American Catholic in North Oak, Pennsylvania was family. It's about the love and the caring that they had for their family. The families were an important part of life growing up back then. Regardless of nationality, it was all about the family. The people were very proud of their family, their heritage, their religion. They will never forget where they came from. It also could very well be that for some strange reason the love some individual or individuals had for their family may have contributed a great deal to one of the strangest murder cases that happened in the 1960's in North Oak, Pennsylvania.

To give you an idea of how this murder shattered the peace of this community you need to have a picture of the typical Italian family of the times. Most of the Italian families from North Oak were content listening to Frank Sinatra, Dean Martin, Perry Como, and just about any male or female Italian singer who was popular at that time. The songs that they may remember listening to were Dean Martin's "Amore" (When the moon hits your eye like a big pizza pie, that's Amore). They loved Frank Sinatra singing "Summer Wind" or "I Got the World on a String", or the "Lady is a Tramp". Then they had the female Italian singer Connie Francis singing "Lipstick on Your Collar". Their favorite comic singer was Lou Monte singing "Pepino the Italian Mouse" or what some would like to call the Italian anthem which was the "Tarantella". Some parents would put on the Italian record albums and dance in the living room of their new houses to the music of the "Tarantella" and "Oh, Marie".It's not hard to understand how these murders shook an entire community that was used to a peaceful life.

2 More Than One

It was 3:15pm on a Monday afternoon when Tony walked into the office of the police station. Detective Tony Lupo is a slender man about six feet tall. He is well groomed, has thick brown hair that is neatly combed back. He is in his early to mid forties and is well dressed. He is a man who is always in a sport coat, neatly pressed slacks, a clean button-down shirt, a necktie that accents whatever colore attire he is wearing on any given day. One of the most important parts of his attire that would support his detective work is his 38 revolver strapped on the left side of his hip. No matter what he wears, he always looks very professional. He comes from a working class Italian American background and has some knowledge in the Italian superstition known as the Malocchio or The Evil Eye. He's been on the North Oak Police Department for over15 years, working his way up from beat cop walking the streets of North Oak to desk sergeant at the Main Street police station, and finally to detective.

Anthony Lupo, commonly known as Tony, is a kind man who loves his wife and children. He has a good work ethic and tries to keep everything in perspective with his Catholic family values. When Lupo's not working trying to solve a murder case, a suicide, a robbery, or a rape, he tries to spend time with his wife Cathy, his daughter Jennifer, and his sons Anthony Jr, and Michael. He enjoys talking sports and playing football, baseball, or basketball in the backyard of their house. He lives in a modest neighborhood in a single colonial four bedroom house in Plymouth

Township. His son Anthony, obviously named after Tony's father and Lupo himself, is six years old and is a bright boy and like his detective father wants to grow up and become a policeman. His daughter Jennifer is nine years old and loves sports. His youngest son Michael is over a year old. Anthony is a very good student in school and a very determined football player in the midget league football team at St. Francis Catholic school. Tony was a young boy when he and his family came to North Oak, Pennsylvania from Caltanissetta, Italy in the late 1930's. He came from Italy with his father Salvatore Lupo, his mother Vivian Rubio,his older brother Salvatore and his younger sister Marianne.

Detective Tony Lupo sat down at his desk and began reading through the local newspaper.

"Yo, Tony, what the hell is up with you?" asked his partner Chubbs" "You walk in, don't say shit to anybody, no hello, or how are you doing, drop dead,... nothing what's up your ass?"

James McFadden, better known as Chubbs, is Tony's partner in crime. Chubbs is a pudgy fella who also wears a sportcoat, slacks, and a shirt that usually hangs past his waistline. His sport coat is never buttoned and his tie is two inches above his belt. Chubbs is about 5 foot 8 inches tall with sandy blonde hair, a round face, and red nose. He is as Irish looking as they come; and needless to say, Chubbs doesn't miss many meals. Whenever Chubbs talks, whether it's a wisecrack, a smart remark, or just typical conversation, he always chuckles at the end of the sentence.

"I'm sorry, Chubbs, I'll tell you what's up my ass, it's a why."

"A why? What the hell do you mean a why?"

"A why is how come nobody knew this evil eye murder could happen."

"Tony we been over this a thousand times. Nobody knew and nobody wanted to talk about it remember? People were scared. Anyway, Tony, I thought we were over all this Mollachia bullshit?"

"It's Malocchio not Mallachia, and no we are not over it. Listen, Chubbs, I've been doing some research, and I found out that some old Italian lady back about ten or twelve years ago was on trial with John Volpe's father for a money deal that she tried to swindle from old man Volpe. We need to follow up on this. We may get some more information that could help us out, not just with this case but maybe on some other cases that were not solved. Now, tomorrow morning you and I are going over to the North Oak *Times* and talk with some folks and try to get a heads up on this story."

"Tony, do you really want to open up this can of worms again? I mean what do you think we are going to find out? The case is closed, it's over. We caught the guy, he's in jail. The end."

Lupo looked up from his desk and sat back a little farther in his chair and said, "Did we, Chubbs, did we really catch the right person for the evil eye murders? I wonder. Remember something, Chubbs; **Most children will do what they're told, as long as someone tells them what to do.**"

"Ok, Tony, now what the hell does that mean?"

"It means let's go out for a while and talk to some people from the press okay?"

"You know something, Tony, it's another thing I don't understand about this Italian superstition. You got the horn that looks like a carrot that you wear around your neck, you got the fingers, the two fingers thing, whatever the hell that means; you get the oil and the water to get rid of the evil spirits. It's all so confusing. How can you or anyone make any sense out of it?"

"Yea, Chubbs, I know what you're saying."

" Remember one thing, Tony, those people were scared, and they believed in superstition. To me it's all bullshit... it's all about the money. I don't think it's about evil spirits. It's about murder money, no evil, alive or dead, or evil fingers or evil whatever the hell it is. It's called murder money, Tony, plain and simple. And the way I see it, you can take that to the bank literally. They want the money because of the price of everything: the price of gas, the price of clothing, the price of food. Everything is going up except my dick."

"You know, Chubbs, almost every nationality that I know has some type of superstitious belief. The Irish, like yourself, believ in leprechauns. The Chinese in the Year of the Dragon or whatever. It goes on and on. I myself, I believe in God. I believe in human beings. You have a good point though, you may be right, it may be murder money, but this evil superstitious belief, the evil eye, is something that I want to follow-up on and get the real murderer and the answer to why he did it or she did it."

"Tony, why can't you just be happy with the end result?"

"Oh, and what is the end result?"

"We caught the son of a bitch, and he is away, and the case is over. Now you want to make a bigger deal out of this and go back years. For what? Sometimes I just don't get you at all."

"Over? Is that what you think, Chubbs, just because we got some guy who said I killed those people, it's over? Well, let me try and explain something to you. Some people can kill and some people would like to have some people killed."

"Tony, what the hell did you just say? There you go again with your Tinker Bell Philosophy That don't mean shit".

"Listen to me. This case goes back a long time, and I am going to get to the bottom of all this bullshit. Ok? Oh and one other thing, Chubbs, I don't mind carrying you, but stop dragging your feet."

"Oh, okay that's real funny, Tony. Did it take you all day to think of that?"

"No, not all day, I just pulled that one out of my ass," he laughed

"Tony, let me be serious for a minute, **ok?** What about this thing being tied to the mafia. You know, we never addressed that issue. I mean that.

We know there's a large mafia presence in Philly,...do you think there could be some mafia action up here?"

"You know, as crazy as it seems, the thought did enter my mind, but this isn't a mafia job. I think this is a revenge job. Besides the mafia has been pretty quiet down the city lately. Between you and me, I did contact a guy I went to high school with. He is a detective and works at the 9th Street station down near Ninth and Catherine Streets. He does a lot of undercover work. It is a new thing, a task force that looks into some of the gambling, prostitution, drugs, and murders that goes on with the mob and the mafia down that area. This guy is the kind of guy you want to have on your team. He was one crazy son of a bitch in high school, and his balls are as big as the Empire State Building."

"What's his name, Tony, and how the hell do you know him?"

"We were good friends in school. We had a lot of fun. We also kinda liked the same type of girls, and we both knew we wanted to be in law enforcement when we got out of school. We were on the football team together. He was one hell of a football player. He would run into people to get tackled just to knock them down. Then we would go back to the huddle and he'd tell me that guy who tackled him was a punk and he could not tackle for shit. He would tell me he was going to run over the next son of a bitch who tries to get him down, and you want to know something, Chubbs, he did. He ran right over the guy going for a touchdown.

"Back then I really don't remember anything about crime let alone murders. I remember as a kid the good times growing up in and around North Oak and Green Hill. It was fun back then. I know I was a kid in grade school, but I didn't know or hear anything about an evil eye, or about a Sicilian curse, or any type of evil. To me and my family and the people we knew back then, it was the good and happy times. I remember guys like my father, his brother, his friends, good men. Like Uncle Salvatore, Charles, Tony, Ninzi and Carlo. I remember more of all the old timers that hung around the Italian American Club. A club that was like a family.

"Some of these guys went out on a Friday night to the club to drink, to laugh about old times, and to play cards or shoot shuffleboard. But I believe the most favorite game that they ever played was the game called Mora, the fingers game. You get two guys and they throw out their fingers with one hand and count from 1 to 5 in Italian. The whole time they were throwing out their fingers they would call out in Italian the numbers. For instance, number one would be uno, number two would be due. number three would be tre, and so on. See back then they were simple games, a simple life, and simple times. No murders, evil spells, superstition, voodoo, or any of that bullshit Those guys are men that were from the second World War and brought up around the Depression. Men who believed in God, Country and Family. Men who work at the local steel company, Allen Wood Steel. Some of the men worked for General Electric. Some were police officers, and some of them either dropped out of school or only had a high school education and that was it. They didn't have time to think up any kind of mysterious or evil bullshit to put a curse on someone. They were too busy making a living for their families. The family back then meant everything to people because when you come down and think about it, that's all they had. But the one thing you can count on, they all loved to laugh. These guys smoked maybe a pack of cigarettes or more a day; Camels, Lucky Strike, Chesterfield, Old Gold. Guys who liked Marilyn Monroe, Liz Taylor, Jane Mansfield, all the beautiful movie stars from the 40's, 50's and 60's. If you were fortunate enough back in the 40's or 50's to have the presence of a mother in the family, that was an extra bonus. She was the lady who kept everything in the household under control. She was the lady of the household that the husband or the children could'nt do without. Mom is the ones that has a heart of gold. Just don't get her angry at you. If you would get out of line, by cursing, by using a bad word, or if you would talk back to Mom, then believe me, she had a hand of steel and it hit real hard. Yeah, it's true. I know my mother and my friend's mothers back then they didn't need to put a curse on you or an evil spell. What you got was a slap or a kick in the ass, and that got your attention. Yes, it was the ladies in the families, the mothers who cooked the dinner and the suppers for their husbands. For their children they made sure that they had a good breakfast in the morning and wore the proper clothes to school. She would talk about classroom studies and playing in

the school yard. That's how it was with most people in this town growing up in the 40's, 50s. It was all about family. It did not matter what
you're heritage was. Italian, Irish, Polish, German, Slovak, a white person or a black person. Growing up back then was simply a great life. See
back then it was all about the family. Good or bad, happiness or sadness,
right or wrong. Wherever, whatever, whoever, it was always about the
family. Your family, my family, everyone's family. All about family and
that was it. You know what I am saying, Chubbs, you lived it too."

"Okay, Tony, it's nice going down Memory Lane with you. I also understand and agree with you about family, but we need to stick to the case.
Maybe tomorrow after we talk with the folks at *The Times* you can call
your buddy Bob Salvi to see if there was any mob action on this side. I
got to go now, I have to get home to my family. I'll see you tomorrow.
Have a good night."

"Okay. Tell Patty and the kids I was asking,... have a good night."

Lupo pushed back in his chair. It rolled across the office hardwood floor
stopping at the center of his oak desk. He leaned back in his chair, folded his hands behind his head, and started to reminisce about his high
school days and his friend Bob Salvi. Life was so simple then. Lupo
wanted to go back in time, but in his mind his curiosity had the better
of him now. He now started to think about not only the murderer, John
Volpe, but about his own self worth. Lupo could not live with himself if the wrong person was behind bars. What if someone else killed
these people, or what if someone helped him kill these people. Maybe
someone put John Volpe up to this and gave him money to say he did
the murders when in reality he did not do it. Lupo knew his mind was
racing, a man can only do so much before he gets burned out. Lupo's
thoughts were going back and forth from the murder scenes to the killer
himself. He did not want to feel any remorse, sorrow, or guilt for the
killer, but he had a strange feeling about this guy John Volpe. He knew
he couldn't solve all the problems of the world, but the world is not the
evil eye. He just wanted to make some type of sense out of this.

3 News: Good or Bad

Detective Lupo parked the car in the parking lot of the local newspaper, *The Times.* The two decetives got out of the car and walked into the reception area of the building.

"Good morning, gentlemen, can I help you?" asked a soft voiced. It was a very attractive blonde who was sitting behind a desk with the sign on the wall behind her that said Information.

"Yes, miss, my name is Detective Lupo and this is Detective McFadden from the North Oak Police Department, and we are here to see Bill Pastino. Could you please let him know we are here?"

The receptionist picked up the phone and said, "Mr. Pastino, you have two genetlemen here to see you." Okay, gentleman take the elavetor to the fourth floor. Mr. Pastino's office is on the right, two doors down, room 223."

The newspaper building was in the center of town off of Main and Second Streets. It was built in the early 1900's with very fine architecture. The front and sides of the building were stone; the wooden staircases was made of mahogany and oak wood. There was hard wood flooring throughout the building. The elevator was the old-fashioned type that had the black sliding-cage door across the front of it.

Bill Postino, was the editor-in-chief, he was a short, stocky fellow with thick black hair and a mustache. He wore a white shirt, a bow-tie, and had a cigar hanging out of the side of his mouth. He had short stubby fingers and looked more like the local butcher instead of an editor of the local paper. He was sitting on a high back chair with a beautiful brown mahogany desk in front of him.

"Good morning, gentlemen, would you like some coffee?"

"No thank you, Bill," Lupo said. "We don't want to take up much of your time.We'd just like to ask you a few questions if you don't mind."

"You said this was important, Detective, but you we're very vague on the phone. What is it you want from me? What can I do for you?"

"Remember several years ago—well over 15 years to be exact— the family feud between two families that was going on over money, power, and superstition. Back then the people in town called it the "evil eye." The case involved a man named John Volpe and a lady named Josephina Silica".

Pastino said, "I remember it well."

"Now we are opening the murder investigation of the five people who were murdered over the past six years. People in the town are closed - mouth about that case, and no one wants to talk to us. It seemed that most of the people were scared or frightened of this "evil eye" superstition. Mc Fadden and I are here to question you to see if you can shed some more light on the subject of these murders. Myself...I'm having a hard time understanding if this feud and superstition began almost 10 years before the first murder, and why didn't anyone know of this type of crime?"

" Let me be clear on this issue, Tony," said Mr. Pastino as he pushed his chair away from the desk, and leaned back crossed his legs, and folded his arms across his chest. He chuckled, shook his head back and forth and said, "I remember this story like it was yesterday. I was a new reporter for the paper back then, and my managing editor sent me out to run with it. Josephina Silica was a healer of sorts, someone who could cure a person of a certain type of illness."

"Excuse me, for interrupting you, but I have a question. Was she along the lines of a nurse or some type of medical doctor, someone of that sort?"

"No, nothing along those lines. She was not a professional. Fom what I gathered, she had special powers that at the time the people in the area believed she could heal. She was somebody that could make you feel better, someone who could make you understand that she was doing good for you. Josephine Silica was some kind of mystical person. She was a lady who made her own medical potions. She could cure a person of headaches, colds, fevers, and chills, almost anything that ailed a person. I wanted to find out what the hell was going on. I wanted to know what all this evil eye" curse was about. Also, some people in town believed that you could give the "evil eye to someone simply by sticking out a fist and two fingers, the index and pinky, you could put the curse on them. That type of gesture was called the Devil's horns. There were people back then - and probably even now - who also believed that a person could not receive the Malocchio, the Evil Eye - just by wearing certain charms or medallions around their neck. One popular amulet was the Italian horn. Some people even wear it today. It is believed to ward off any type of evil that may come your way."

" I'd like to ask you about the special powers that you mentioned. Were they all good special powers?"

" It was well known around town that Josephina Silica was a lady to be respected or feared... period."

"I don't think she was as respected as much as she was feared."

"Ah, yes, how correct you are, a man of interest and knowledge. I like that because knowledge in this case could very well be an important advantage. I can tell you this: There may be some old archives from our newspaper that may be kept, if I'm not mistaken, in the North Oak Library. I do believe you may find some information dating back to the 1950's about this case. It may help you to draw some conclusions that may back up your interest. If I'm not mistaken, it started with an amount of money. I believe it was around $10,000. Apparently, Mr. Volpe was accusing Mrs. Silica of swindling him out of this money. From what I can remember, I believe that was how the whole thing started. Now, would you call it loansharking, money laundering, or simply stealing or taking money, I don't know, What I do know is back in 1950 $10,000 was a lot of money to people in our town. What the hell, Detective, $10,000 is a lot of money today, so I'm sure you could understand what made it interesting news and it sold a lot of our newspapers. Apparently, a lot of people back then were interested not only in the two people involved but were interested because of the amount of money involved, how it started, and how it ended. It's a simple fact, some people are attracted to another person's demise. And that fortunately for us or unfortunately for the people involved, we sell a lot of newspapers, and that's the bottom line to sell the newspapers and tell the story as truthfully and with as much information as we have at our disposal. I would like to talk with you some more on this case, but I do have an important meeting in ten minutes.

"Thanks for your time Bill. Yes, I'd like to continue this conversation at some other time. Again thank you for your time and have a good day."

Back at the police station Tony and Chubbs were in the office for almost a good half of the day going over some pieces of news from *The Times* that they got from the library. They found out that the Volpe family was being set up by an older Italian lady from the area. It was a very interesting story that had to deal with the superstition and money. The story dated back to the early 1950's. Through their research they found out that the suspect's father at that time was a 46-year-old jeweler, a watchmaker. He had given almost $10,000 to Josephine Silica who was to cure Mr. Volpe of some medical ailments that he had.

Tony and Chubbs were both interested in the findings of that case. They both realized that they wanted to do more research dating back to 1950. They wanted to continue but knew that they would have to put it off until Monday morning; it was almost the end of the day on a Friday afternoon and they both knew that they gave it all they could this week.

"Look, Chubbs, it's almost quarter to five. What do you say we wrap this thing up for the weekend and hit it hard Monday. I got to get going anyway, my nephews is playing football tonight over at Campbell Field. Cathy and I are going to go see the game. I think it starts at 7 o'clock. I got to get home, shower, eat dinner, get the kids set, and get to the game. I better get the hell out of here."

"Oh, your nephew's playing football tonight. Who is he playing for and who are they playing?"

"It's my sister-in-law Donna's son Michael. He plays quarterback for Saint Anthony's High School, and I think they're playing St. Matt's from Wayne."

"Okay, Tony, enjoy the game. Have fun and have a good weekend. I'll see you Monday morning."

"Okay, Chubbs, tell the family I was asking for them and thanks for your help this week. I'll see you Monday."

As Lupo was leaving the police station and walking to his car, he heard some commotion on the south end of the station at the back side corner of the grocery store. As he walked closer to investigate the commotion, he noticed four white teenage boys who were giving two black boys some trouble. As he walked around the corner, he noticed that the white youths were older then the two black youths, and they were spitting, calling them names, and pushing them around. As Tony got closer, he noticed one of the boys picked up a soda bottle from the ground and was going to throw it and hit one of the black kids with the bottle. Tony was only about five feet away from the commotion, and he said to the one youth with the bottle, "What the hell are you guys doing?" The youth with the bottle turned around and said to Tony, "Get the hell out of here. This is none of your business." It was at that time Lupo walked over to the boys and confronted them.

"Listen to me. I'm a cop. You want to jerk around with somebody? I will throw your ass in jail. Now put the bottle down."

"Listen, you don't understand these Niggers don't belong up here. We want them out of here and we want to straighten them out, you know show them who's boss."

"You watch your mouth, boy. There is no need to be calling them names. Now keep your mouth shut before I put my foot up your ass. **Do you understand that?** You punks don't understand a thing. I was around the corner and heard everything. I know everything that was going on and saw what you tough guys, you four big tough guys, were doing to these two kids. You guys were breaking their balls because you don't like black kids."

"Hey, listen PAL, you don't understand there's **FOUR** of us and **ONE** of you, and how do we know if you're cop or not. You could be just some jerk off just jerking us around."

"Listen to me all of you. I got a badge. See I got a gun right on my side. I may be one man, but I'm a cop."

"Yeah, with two other cops behind him. So now you see, you punks, the way we look at it, it's four against three and we like them odds," came a voice behin Tony.

It was just at that moment Tony turned around and saw two black officers standing right behind him. He knew the two police officer from his station. The one man was Officer Robert Smith and the other officer was Don Baker. Tony greeted them with a smile, shaking his head as he turned around laughing and said to the four boys, "I got a bad feeling that you four fellows just got your asses a room at the station for the night. So I want you four tough guys to stand against the wall, spread your legs, and I'm sure that these two fine police officers we'll be more than glad to frisk you and take your names so you can call your parents and inform them that you got a room for the night at our station."

With that Tony walked over to the two young black kids to see if they were okay. The two boys assured Tony that they were not hurt and that they were all right. They asked Tony if it was okay if they went home now. Tony informed the boys that the two officers would take them home, and they would be safe. He reassured the boys that the four white fellas will not give them anymore trouble; and if they have anymore problems with anyone, he told the boys to give him a call. Tony handed the boys his card. He then walked over to Officer Smith and asked him to radio for a car to take the two young boys home. Tony then noticed that the officers already had all four youths in cuffs.

Officer Baker was a tall, well-built man who stood about six foot five inches tall. He was a light skinned man with a flat top crewcut. He had been a football and basketball star athlete in high school. He also was awarded a football scholarship at Villanova University. He was the type of man who spoke intelligently and softly, but he carried a big stick. Needless to say, the four white boys did not give Officer Smith or Officer Baker any trouble at all. Officer Baker walked over to Tony and informed him that he had smelled alcohol on their breath, and two of the boys were carrying switch blades. Tony looked at Officer Baker and asked him to step around the back of a police car so they could talk.

"Listen, I want you to take these four idiots in to the station, confiscate their weapons, then call their parents. Sergeant Cannon is on duty tonight. He will know exactly what to do with these four idiots and how to handle their parents. Between me and you, I don't think they'll spend the night in jail, but at least Sargent Cannon we'll give them a hard time and he will let their parents know what went on."

After Tony told officer Baker what to do, Officer Smith came around to the back of the patrol car to talk to Tony.

"Detective Lupo, I just got off the horn with Officer Riley; he's on his way over to pick up the two boys to take them home."

"Okay, thank you. I just informed Officer Baker about these four idiots and what to do and to let Sergeant Cannon handle the situation back at the station. I also want to thank both of you for having my back. I want both of you to know I won't forget it. Officer Baker, if I'm not mistaken, I think you are up for taking the sergeant exam, am I correct?"

"Yes, Detective Lupo, you are correct."

"I'll put it in a good word for you. I'll speak to the chief and tell him about what happened tonight, and that you both had my back and were a big support for me."

"Thank you. Officer Smith and I appreciate it, but we were really just doing our job. I would like to commend you on the job that you did and the other detectives from our department did to solve the "evil eye" murders. I got to tell you that from our side of the fence some of my people we're scared and concerned especially that it's one thing about the five murders, but it also was getting people frightened about the superstitious belief. I think that a lot of us from the department were more concerned than people on the outside thought we were. I personally think that the press and what people were reading in the newspaper did more harm than good on this case. This whole damn town was scared and frightened. Not only you white folks, but our community also. I mean, I just can't figure how it took almost six years and five murders to catch this guy."

"I thank you for the compliment; but believe me, I had a lot of help and was not the only one on this investigation. I had some good people helping me, and I agree with you that almost six years was a long time to catch a killer."

"You know something, Detective Lupo, it's a good thing when we can all work together. I enjoy my job and what I do, and I want you to know it's damn good working with people of your caliber. I want to thank you again for anything you can do for us."

The two men shook hands and thanked each other again as they went on their separate ways.

4 Looking for a Home

When the Lupo family arrived in the United States from Italy, they lived with Tony's father's older brother Albert Lupo and his family for a period of nine months. Salvatore Lupo was a barber by trade, and within nine months he had moved his family from his brother Albert's home into their first house on Buttonwood Street and opened up his barber shop on Fornance Street. Salvatore Lupo, Detective Lupo's father, did not understand why some of the people that he knew, such as his wife's family or their friends, would call him crazy for leaving Italy for America. Salvatore Lupo wanted the chance to make a better life for his family. He wanted the opportunity that he felt was his one and only chance to bring them to America. He was sincere in his belief of what he must do for himself and his family. It would be their future way of living. He had the vision as so many other immigrants had, that America was truly the land of opportunity.

In fact, that was the way Salvatore Lupo Sr. was thinking at that time before he, his wife Vivian,and his three small children left the southern section of Italy, the inner part of Sicily in the town of Caltanissetta. Caltanissetta is a rural village located far from the coastline in the center of the Sicilian hinterland. It's a rich producer of wheat. In this town it is a known fact that the landowners and farmers abandoned their countryside and became miners. Salvatore Lupo's father was a miner who worked very rigorously in the mines. In the 19th century Caltanissetta was considered the world capital of sulfur and exported the mineral to all industrialized countries.

One late night on the ship traveling from Italy to America, a man snuck up on Salvatore while he was sleeping and put his hand on the back of his head. He tried to force Salvatore down onto his crotch. They struggled and Salvatore bit the man's hand. The man yelled out, and at that moment a large man with a beard came over and grabbed the man and pulled him off of Salvatore. He put a knife to the mans throat and said, "If you brother this man again, I will cut your eyes out and feed them to the fish, you bastard." He pushed the man down and kicked him.

Salvatore was grateful to this man who had saved him from a very uncomfortable situation and reached out his hand in the gesture of thanks. The two men shook hands and spoke Italian, exchanging conversation asking each other if everything was okay now. The man who helped Salvatore was Carlo Vanbessai whose family owned a fish market in Sici-ly. He explained to Salvatore that he had to leave Italy to get away from some bad people. Carlo did not have to elaborate more on why he was leaving Italy and the kind of people he was running from. Salvatore un-derstood the kind of people he was talking about. Carlo was to meet his father's brother, his uncle Bruno, who lived in Brooklyn, New York and owned a construction business. He wrote down on a piece of paper his name, his uncle's name, and the name of his construction business. He told Salvatore that if he ever needed anything to come and see him for any help at all. He told him that he was a good man and could tell he had a wonderful family. Salvatore Lupo knew he had made a good friend. They exchanged information, and Carlo assured him that they would be in touch. Carlo and Salvatore stayed together talking about Italy and what life may be like in America. It seemed that both men had made a good bond. Salvatore knew now why he had made the journey. He felt at peace with himself and the feeling of success, of freedom, of hope. To him a whole new world was about to open up. They actually stayed in touch with one another through the years. Salvatore and Carlo would visit one another's families periodically. Salvatore was godfather to one of Carlo's children, and Carlo was godfather to one of Salvatore's children. Also Carlo's and Salvatore,s children showed their respect by calling them uncle and aunt whenever they were celebrating holidays with their families. As a young child Lupo always enjoyed going up to New York City to visit his Uncle Carlo and his family.

The immigrants who came to America needed to proceed out into a new day. A new beginning was about to happen, not just for the people who were born in America but for everyone who was and became an American. The American society and families were ready for a change, the people were hungry for a change, for a better life, and a good time. Give them the baseball games, the picnics in the parks, a cold beer, a hot dog, and a damm good hamburger. Hail to the RED WHITE AND BLUE.

Salavtore's older brother, Antonio Lupoand his wife worked hard in America. They were not wealthy people, but they gave their children a good Catholic upbringing, and Salavtore did the same. They put a roof over their heads and food on the table. Spaghetti was for dinner at least two or three days a week. On Sunday they always had to have a nice spaghetti dinner with fresh baked bread and a good garden salad. The family would always eat dinner together. They tried to show their children that you don't get anything for free in this world, that anything worth getting is worth working for. They tried to show them right from wrong. To put a roof over their heads.

Salvatore loved his older brother Antonio and looked up to him. They would work hard, but they would laugh even harder. The men would gamble, play cards, smoke, and stay up late into the night.

Back in the 1950's and 60's in the town of North Oak it was true that there were some bad and strange people. Some people who believed in old wives tales, such as the evil superstition that would cause harm or sickness to an individual. Like any town there were the bad and strange people, but then there were the good and very nice people, people who just wanted to be helpful and enjoy life. That special time in life the men wore hats and the woman wore dresses. Chevy, Ford, Buick, Pontiac, and Oldsmobile were the cars to drive. Gas was 19 cents a gallon. Girls and boys loved to dance to rock and roll. Yes, the 1950's were here, the people loved their homes, their cars, their schools, and their families. Hell, they even liked the neighbor next door. There was a luncheonette that made a sandwich called a zep that was made only at this one store in Lupo's hometown. It only had provolone cheese, a bermuda onion, tomato, lunchmeat, and oil. The thing that made the sandwich really good was that the bread was a good Italian roll. The bread was from Tacico Italian bakery. There were a lot of good bakeries in and around the towns. They also had a great tomato pie that was made at Rosellio Italian Market. Back then you could buy a pie for $2.50, and it could feed about 10 people. The Lupo family always got one or two pies whenever there was a Holy Communion or a confirmation or any type of family party or picnic. The tomato pie was the big treat at any family gathering. It was all about the times, faith, families and love. And so it was hard to believe that the evil eye could be a part of this almost perfect world.

5 The Sins Of Society

It was about 8:15 PM on Thursday night, Lupo and Chubbs were working a little late. Chubbs said to Tony, "I'm getting out of here. I'm done for today. The wife is making her famous Irish stew, and I don't want to miss it for anything. Are you going home now or you going to hang around for a while?"

"I'm going to take a ride for a bit, then I'm heading home. I'll see you tomorrow, Chubbs, have a good night and tell Patty and the kids I said hello."

As Tony was leaving the police station and walking to his car, he thought to himself, *I don't know if I even want to go any further on this murder case. I need to get some help on this end and find out what's up.*

The next day, Friday morning, Tony walked into the station wanting to ask McFadden a question. As Tony was looking in Chubb's direction getting ready to ask him the question, Chubb's was already looking and talking to Tony. "This guy Volpe who is accused of the murders, what a sick son of a bitch he is. This guy is a wack-a-doodle. Why the hell are we still working on this case, Tony? I mean what the hell is up with this bullshit?"

Tony knew that Chubbs was right. It seemed like they were just spinning their wheels round and round and round. "I know it's hard, and I know we've been doing this for a long time. I'd just like to see if you can hang in there with me because I got something on my mind."

"What's on your mind?"

"This guy admitted he did the killing, and we've been working at this through the six years and five murders from 1961 on. I just have one question that's been bothering me for a long time. This evil eye curse thing happened back in 1950 between the father from the Volpe family and this lady Josephine Silica right?"

"Yea, you're right. So what's bothering you?"

"Why the hell didn't we see it or anyone else see it and go back to review this case from the 1950's? Nobody, Chubbs,... I mean not one damn soul probably even knew or thought about going back to 1950 about this evil eye case that these two people were involved in. I mean maybe there could have been some way that some lives could have been saved if you know what I mean?"

"Tony, we talked about this before. Nobody was killed back then with all this bullshit about evil spirits, the Malocchio, the horns, and all that crap. I guess nobody thought it could lead to five people getting killed. You know, Tony, you and I broke our balls trying to solve this case. The department worked hard on this. When you're in a small town and people don't want to talk to the police because they're scared shitless, what the hell else can we do?

"You're right. When I think about it, we got some sick son of a bitches in this town. I mean who in their right mind picks up a 16-year-old girl, rapes her, cuts off one of her breasts, and shoves a Coke bottle up her, and swears he had nothing to do with it?"

"Tony, on the Carri Anne Twitchell case, you weren't on that by yourself, were you? Refresh my memory?"

"That was a disgusting case. I remember when I got the call. I was home with the family and I got a call from Lieutenant Murphy. He tells me that some girl from Stoneborough had been missing for two days, and the police down there needed some support from our department. It all happened about a year before the evil eye murders".

"I had to go down to Stoneborough and talk to one of the detectives on the case; his name was Paul Gallo or something like that. He was a tall skinny guy with the pencil - point mustache, and I remember he smoked Old Gold cigarettes. When I got into the office, he told me that they were looking at a suspect from Green Hill a guy name Vincent Jones. I remember that I no sooner got into his office and we were sitting there talking about the case and his phone rang. It was his captain and he wanted to talk to us. He said he had a lead on the case and that they had found the girl's body. So Gallo and I got up there right away.

"You know something, Chubbs, I can remember this case like it happened yesterday, and then there's other times when it seems like it was so far away and a long time ago. This girl was only 16, a beautiful girl from a beautiful family, and this son of a bitch had to kill her. Not only did this prick kill her, he mulated her. He cut off one of her breasts, shoved a Coke bottle up her vagina, then shoved the twig up her rectum, and left her naked in the woods in a field to die like a animal. I know we're police officers and we got to be tough and strong, and we have to deal with this type of violence. Well, this poor girl didn't deserve this type of destiny. Like I said, there were about two or three detectives and police officers at the scene, and I don't think there was a dry eye among any of us."

Chubbs could tell by the look on Tony's face that he was having a hard time. Tony was a sincere, thoughtful, honest, goodhearted man. He also knew he was having a hard time talking and dealing with this type of case. Chubbs thought to himself, *I worked with Tony for years and I never saw this side of him. I never saw how the darkness and horrible, despicable actions could bring an honest good man to tears.*

"How are you doing, Tony, are you okay?"

"Yeah, I'm okay. It's just that some cases you just never get over. Detective Gallo and I and the other detectives and police officers stood there in the damp, foggy, overcast day as this poor young girl lay there on the ground naked. This evil bastard should go to hell for what he did to this girl."

At that moment the sensitive side of Detective Anthony Lupo came out and he started to choke up as tears ran down his face.

"You know something, Chubbs, this brutal case happened around the same time as the "Evil Eye Murders." I've investigated and I've seen my share of murder cases but for some reason, this little 16-year-old girl brutally raped, sodomized, and cut up like an animal just did something to me. I'm sorry for letting my emotions get the best of me now. I think it's time we get this day started."

Lupo knew that he was having a hard time. He also understood that there would be some point in his life when a murder case would get to him. It seemed like the Carry Ann Twitchell case was bringing the darkness into his mind. Whenever Lupo would think of this case, it would be like dark black shadows in his mind. Not only was this shadow dark, it was heavy. It was weighing very heavily on his mind. It was like he was running down a long, dark hallway thinking to himself, *I need to save this girl. I need to save her life. This girl is too young to die. This could be my own daughter.* There were doors all along the hallway. Tony tried each door, trying to get out of the hallway and save that girl, but every door was locked. Then there were times, not many, but there were times when he would think that maybe it was time for him to quit the force, to retire. It may be too much for him. *STOP,* he thought to himself. *What the hell am I thinking? I like this type of work, and I also like getting the scum off the streets,* but the Carry Ann Twitchell case was something that would always be in the back of his mind.

Talking about the case just brought it back to reality for a short time. To Lupo it was like putting it at the bottom drawer of the filing case and locking it. He loved his wife, he loved his children, and he knew that he was a good father and a good husband. He wanted to provide the best things in life he can give. Thinking to himself, he utters in the quiet of his own mind *I wish I could've saved you. I'm sorry I wasn't there for you. God bless you, Carry Ann Twitchell, wherever you are.*

6 Sunday Dinner

I t was the weekend, and like any weekend in North Oak it was your ordinary Saturday and Sunday. In the Lupo family Tony was trying to spend as much time as he could with his three children. He wanted Saturday morning or afternoon to be their playing time of baseball, football, basketball or whatever the weather at that time permitted. Tony knew that he needed this and had a funny way of putting it: He called it his mental enema. To Tony this was his release from work and all the serious and depressing problems on the police force. It was the time Tony could put away his gun, put his badge in the drawer, put on his sneakers, jeans, and his favorite Philadelphia Phillies baseball hat. Sometimes on a Saturday he would take the family for a day trip to the Philadelphia Zoo or for a picnic at Valley Forge Park. Sundays were sacred: that was when every one from the Lupo family, including Tony's brother and sister; would go over to Tony's parents house for Sunday spaghetti dinner. This was not only a time for Tony's kids to bond with their cousins, it was a time for Tony and his family to laugh, to tell a joke or two, and, yeah, talk about how the Philadelphia teams were doing. There were also times when Tony and his immediate family would spend time over at his wife Cathy's mother and father's house. Cathy and Tony were glad that their children were spending time with both sides of the family.

One Sunday in particular Tony and his family were eating dinner at his mother's and father's house when the conversation changed from sports or new cars to what's going on with the "evil eye" murders. Tony's brother Salvatore poured Tony an after- dinner glass of wine and said to him,"Tony, I hope you don't mind me asking you something about the 'Evil Eye Murder Case.' Almost everybody in town knows one thing or another about that case. I was wondering something about the accused person involved in the killing of the five people. The reason I'm asking is because the other day I happened to run into Louis Russo; he knows that you are my brother and almost everyone knows from the information in *The Times* that you were the lead detective on the murder case. So we were talking, and he asked me if anything was going on further with the case or about the perpetrator himself. I distinctly remember him saying there were a lot of questions about this fellow. People wondered if he was really the one who killed all the people. I hope you don't mind me asking because I am a little curious myself."

"It's funny you should ask, Sal, my partner Chubbs—you know Sergeant Michael McFadden, everybody calls him Chubbs That is the name he goes by now and he seems to be good with that. Anyway, we are going over a few aspects of the case."

"Michael McFadden, yeah I remember him, he was about a year behind me in high school. You call him Chubbs, huh?... yeah, as I remember, he was a little chubby in high school. He was a pretty funny guy, always cracking jokes, making fun of people, and other things, you know like the class clown. He was a good guy, everybody liked him."

"Well, I can't tell you everything because of the investigation, but I can tell you that we're just looking into it a little further."

Lupo knew he couldn't say much about the case even though sitting at the table it was just Lupo, his brother, and his father.

The Lupo family in some ways resembled each other. Salvatore, or Sal as he was called by the other members of the family, is a tall fellow, about six foot two with curly, jet black hair and a great personality. He is a good family man and provides well for his family. He studied medicine at Pennsylvania University in Philadelphia and graduated with a medical degree. Sal enjoys the good life and treats people the way he would like to be treated. He is very good to his wife Maureen and loves above all things his two children: his 12-year-old daughter Mary Grace is the love of his life, and his eight-year-old son Salvatore always wants to play baseball and have a catch with his father. Sal, being in the medical field, he doesn't smoke at all and is active in exercising. He keeps his weight at a minimum, although he loves his mom's homemade baked lasagna.

Anthony Lupo Senior, known to the family simply as Dad, is a man of great stature and strength. He stands about five foot eight with grayish white hair and has a receding hairline. His speech is very slow and soft but very accurate. His barbershop is one of the top three in the town and has a very good clientele. Unlike his son Salvatore, Anthony Senior has one bad habit, smoking his little Italian cigars. He's a good man with a great sense of humor and is very old-fashioned in his Italian beliefs that the man provides for his family and must take care of his wife and children. He's in fairly good shape, for a man in his mid to late 60's. He wears glasses that are bifocals, and enjoys his glass of red wine with his dinner.

Lupo's father turned to him and said, "You know, Anthony, this "evil eye" case went back to long before the murders. There was something going on in town with this old lady. I don't remember her name, but I think it was Josephine Silica and the man was the watchmaker Mr. Volpe. He had a jewelry store downtown on Main Street.

"Yeah, we know about that, Dad. What is it that you know or may have heard?"

"Well, I always try to keep in mind the old Italian saying. **Remember one thing: when you point your finger at someone, there are three fingers pointing back at you.** I don't like to talk about people and I don't like gossiping; all I know is from what I hear in the barbershop or from other people around town. Apparently, that lady had some kind of special powers that some people around town believe in."

"Ah that's a bunch of bullshit, Dad. Tony and the police department don't believe in that bullshit. It's all these crazy people in town who believe in that superstition and the evil eye."

"Salvatore, I'm only telling you what I hear, that's all. I am not a smart man like you and Anthony. **I remember when I was a smart, but now I would be smart if I could remember.**" They all laughed.

"Listen, Dad and Tony, I'm only telling you some of the things that I hear, and I'm telling you some of the things I hear may not be true. Tony, from what I remember in the paper, this guy was out to kill seven people and he ended up killing five. Also from what I read in the paper and some of the talk that's out on the street is that it was all about money. Now the way I look at it is that the old Italian people who believe in the Malocchio are going to say it's all about this curse. Some of the younger people and some of the Shylocks and bookies running around this town say it's about the money. I just want to ask you one question: what do you believe?"

"Listen, I understand, I understand both sides of the story. It's just the way it is, and hopefully we got the right person in jail for the crime."

"Another thing I heard in the barbershop and from other people around town is how do you know if the son really killed the people," Lupo's dad said.

"That's exactly what I'm saying." Sal continued, "What Louis Russo was asking me about is what the people in this town are thinking and talking about. The people in this town are so afraid and so goofy about the murders that they will say almost anything just to get some type of a rumor started."

As Lupo's brother and father were conversing about the murders, Tony himself sat there listening and drifting off. He had been working on the murder case almost 24-7. He knew it was his job to think about it five days a week. Did he really wanted to talk about this at a family dinner? *Not really*, he thought to himself. *But if this is what the people in the town must be thinking it may not hurt me to listen.* Tony knew if this is what the people are thinking and if this is what the newspapers are selling, then maybe, just maybe, his thinking about the "evil eye" murders was on the right track. As Tony was thinking to himself, Sal turned to him and brought up another murder case. He questioned Tony about the Carrie Anne Twitchell case.

"Tony, did you hear me? I asked you about the Carrie Anne Twitchell case, the guy from Green Hill who killed that girl."

"I'm sorry, Sal, I was thinking about something. What was it you said to me about the Carrieanne Twitchell case?"

"I was going to say that's a shame about that poor girl. I am aware that she was killed several years ago, but from what I remember she was brutally beaten and molested. I don't know if you can talk about it or if you want to, but sometimes, my brother, I do feel for you. Between you and me, Tony, I don't how you do it. What I'm trying to say is that as a physician when some of my patients or some people that I know are sick and don't have long to live, sometimes it just gets to me. I know that you had some part working on the Carrie Anne Twitchell case, and now you're working on the "Evil Eye" murders again. I guess what I'm trying to say is that what you know and what you see has got to be very difficult. God bless you, my brother, you're a better man than me."

"Yea, my son Anthony, that goes for me too. You always were a good son and a smart man."

Lupo looked to his father and brother and said, "You know, Dad, you are a smart man, and I want to tell you one thing. I say to some of the younger people who I work with, I tell them that. **As I got older my father got a lot smarter**". They laughed together.

"You want to know something, Salvatore and Anthony, since we are talking about this Malocchio murder case and about that poor girl who was murdered in the town of Stoneboro, and because we're talking about loansharking and corruption, let me tell you something about what people do that are involved in the business of lending out money in the old country, as I like to call it. I want to tell you a story that you're Uncle Carlos Vanbessai told me that happened a long time ago in his hometown. It happened right before Carlos and his family left for America. Apparently, in or around his hometown where they lived—I think it was the town called Villalba in Sicily—well, there had been some mafioso trouble in the area. He was telling me about this one family who had been involved in what you call money laundering and loan sharking, that type of business. If I remember correctly, the family Uncle Carlos mentioned had a food business, I believe it was something like a grocery store. Well, from what Carlos told me, they had been in a little financial trouble with some fella who had connections to the Cosa Nostra.

"Excuse me, Dad, for interrupting, but was uncle Carlos ever involved in the Cosa Nostra?"

"No, no, Salvatore. As far as I know, Uncle Carlos was never involved in any of the underworld business. Apparently, Uncle Carlos knew about this guy from one of his cousins. Carlos told me that his cousin knew this guy personally and told him this story. Now whether Carlo's cousins was involved in this type of business, that I do not know.

"Sal, please let dad finish. Ok, Dad, continue your story".

"As I was saying, one day the people with the financial trouble got a visit from this fellow involved in the underworld. The way the story goes is that he went over to their house and talked to the husband and wife and told them that they had one week to come up with the money to pay their debt. They had a little dog that the people, especially the woman, were very fond of. Well, the dog was growling and barking at the man and would not stop. Uncle Carlos told me that this lady would let the dog have the run of their house. Everybody in the town knew how much she loved this dog. She would let the dog go outside in her backyard to go to bathroom. She would wipe the dog's ass after it went to the bathroom; and in the winter time, when it was cold, she would put a little coat to cover the dog to keep it warm. So what happened is a week went by and this couple did not come up with the money. One day when the dog was in the yard going to the bathroom, it disappeared. A few days went by and they could not find the dog. The lady was very upset that she lost her dog. One night late in the evening as the couple was sleeping, they heard a knock at the front door. So the husband and wife went down to answer the door. As they opened the door, the dog was there. He was dead. Stuck to the door with a ice pick. The very next day the people paid their debt in full. You can believe me, my sons, back in the old country if you didn't pay your debt, all hell came down on you. See, the way it was in the old country was first you get a warning. If the warning didn't work, they would kill your pet. Whether it was a dog a cat, whatever. Sometimes they would kill it and leave it on the front door step, or sometimes they would kill it and nail it to the door. If that didn't work, then someone would be murdered. I guess it's possible that the same thing happens here in this country . Whether it's an 'evil eye' curse or somebody's pet is killed or possibaly someone is murdered. That is what happens in the old country, and now it apparently happens here in America."

Tony and his brother looked at one another shaking their heads in disbelief.

"Salvatore, I want you and the two boys to come in here to the living room please. I want to put some music on so we can dance with our grandchildren," Tony's mom said.

"Ok, ok we will be right in. Come on, Salvatore and Anthony, your mother wants us to join them and listen to some music."

As the Lupo men were done talking and the women had finished cleaning up, Tony's mother put on some good Italian music. She put on her favorite Lou Monte album and one of her favorite songs by Lou Monte called the *Tarantella*. The Lupo men looked at each other and started to laugh because they could hear Tony's mother, his wife, his children, his brother Salvatore's wife and children laughing and dancing to the songs. The men sat there at the dining room table just shaking their heads about the story their father had just told them.

"Well, Dad, I guess that's our cue to get in there and dance with the party."

No sooner did Tony say that when a voice from the living room shouted, "Are you guys going to come out and see these kids dance?"

"We're coming, don't worry, we're on our way," one of the men shouted back.

When the men entered the room, Tony's and Sal's wife were dancing with the kids. Tony's mother was also dancing. They all were dancing to the *Tarantella*. Tony and his brother started to dance with the rest of the family. Tony and Sal were dancing with their wives. At various times they would switch back and forth. Tony and Sal also danced with their mother. The kids were laughing. Tony's father was sitting there watching and laughing too. Tony and Sal's wives were laughing, clapping, and enjoying themselves. Tony and Sal we're laughing. Everybody was clapping their hands and laughing and having a good old time. After a couple of minutes of dancing and clapping, Tony's mother dropped her hands and said, "I've had enough!" and sat down next to Tony's father. Tony's mother and father just kept clapping their hands. Tony and Sal were throwing their arms up in the air, putting their hands on their hips, and picking their legs up dancing and dancing. The children really did not know how to do this dance, but no matter what, they were dancing and having a good old time. Actually, Tony and Sal we're doing the dance very traditionally, very simply because they grew up listening to Lou Monte and a lot of the good old favorite Italian music.

After the music was done playing, everyone was laughing, clapping, and just having a family good time. Tony's mother said to everyone, "Just remember our family reunion is coming up soon, and we should all try and make it, so we can have a good time and we can all see your cousins, your aunts, and your uncles. You really will have a lot of fun." The traditional Sunday dinner at the Lupo household was another enjoyable day when the family would laugh, talk about a lot of different things, and just enjoy each other until another week went by. On their way home Tony and Cathy laughed, talked to the kids in the car, and told them how good they were, that they loved them. It simply was a day of good old American family fun. For today, Detective Tony Lupo was not on the job. He was simply a family man. a man, who just wanted to have fun, and he did it today with his family. Tony understood very well that it's all about family.

7 The Watchmaker's Son

On Monday morning Tony Lupo was back at the police station going over some local reports when the chief of police called up to Lupo's desk to tell him he wanted to see him and Chubbs in his office. The police chief of the North Oak police department was a man named Emery Francis Ryder. He stood about 5 feet 9 inches and was a stocky built fellow. He had thick reddish hair and word dark black-rimmed glasses. He was sitting behind his desk on a chair that had wheels that move back forth and side to side. As he sat there leaning back on his chair, he had a habit of tapping on the top of his desk with a number two pencil and eraser. Whenever he would start talking, he would start tapping on his desk with a pencil. As he was leaning back and tapping on his desk, he asked, "So, Tony, how are you doing with this 'Evil Eye Murder Case?' Have you gotten any more information that we can go over or that we can talk about. What's going on with the son, the accused who is incarcerated?"

"Well, Chief, it's like this…"

"Drop the Chief stuff, Tony, it's Frank to you, okay?"

"**Frank**…. I thought your name was **Emery.** Where did Frank come from?"

"Emery is the name on my birth certificate. I am named after my mother's father, okay? My full name is Emery Francis Ryder, so I always used my middle name Frank. What are you laughing at, Chubbs? You like that name Emery don't you?" Chubbs was sitting off to the side laughing to himself as the chief and Tony we're joking and laughing about the chief's first name, he spoke up and said, "Hey, hold on, Chief, I'm staying out of this one. Tony's doing all the talking and asking questions, not me."

"Well, Frank, let me ask you a question: How is it when you and I were in the luncheonette having lunch that day Blanche, the waitress, used the name Emery when she said you were harmless. How in the hell did she know your first name was Emery? She didn't call you Frank if I'm not mistaken."

"That's easy to answer. See, Blanche and I were talking about her name and that was when she informed me that Blanche was not her real name. Her real name is— well, if I tell you, please don't call her by her real name— her real first name is Beatrice. So I told her my real first name was Emery. To be honest with you, when Blanche and I are kind of flirting around, you might say, we call each other by our given first names. Now, if you two fellas are happy and enjoy that, can we now get down to business?"

"Ok, Frank, as I was saying, it's like this: I believe we may have the killer in custody, but from what we're finding out, he's got an attorney and I believe he may want to use the insanity plea."

"What are you saying, Tony? That you do not believe we have the killer? It sounds like you're not sure or you're thinking it maybe someone else involved."

"There just may be some other family members from his family involved."

"Oh, yeah, who you got in mind, Tony?"

" Chief, if I may interrupt for minute please."

"Yeah, Chubbs, what's on your mind?"

"Tony and I have been working this case for a while now, as you know. There is or was some speculation that the father may have been involved. We don't know."

"Is that what you guys are thinking, Tony?"

"Chubbs is right. We'd like to stay with this case just to see what we come up with, just to make sure we have the right person. We found out that the son was in the service but he left on some technicality. I'm not sure of the correct verbiage, but we believe it was some thing psychiatric."

"Or maybe the son is smarter than we think he is. What do you guys think about that? Tell me Tony, Chubbs, do you think he's a smart guy or am I just shooting from the hip? Listen, you two guys, as far as I'm concerned you two are doing a good job. I want to believe that we have the right person in jail. Now that he lawyered up and is taking this insanity plea, you two guys can stay on this case and keep me informed as you go along. Listen, I'm not going to bug you or I'm not going to break your balls, just let me know every once in a while what the hell's going on. I trust you guys. I know you two do good work. Now, is there anything else that you can tell me about this case?"

"One thing for sure, Frank, is during our investigation, Chubbs and I found out he had seen a psychiatrist. He had a list, as you know of seven people that he wanted exorcised of evil spirits. Now, the way we're thinking is he either thought that this would maybe be his ace in the hole card to play on the insanity case, or he was showing somebody the list of people he was going to kill to help him with the insanity plea."

" Some of what you're saying makes sense, I'll give you guys that."

"During our investigation Chubbs and I had found out the son is kind of a weird fella. In other words, he was shy, quiet, and mostly kept to himself. Now that doesn't make him the bad guy or even a killer, but sometimes, especially in the old-fashioned Italian way, some children do what they're told."

"I think I understand what you are saying. You know most children will do what they're told as long as someone tells him what to do."

"From what Chubbs and I found, the son listens to and obeys the father. He was also very close to his mother. I'm not saying he was a mama's boy, I'm just saying he really watched out for his mother. From what we're hearing from the people that we interviewed, he was basically pretty much a loner. We interviewed some other people at his place of employment in town here. It's called the J and D Box company. Some of the people say he was very weird. Some of the people said they really didn't like him, that they were scared of him."

"Well, Tony, what do you think these people are going to say? They're not going to say they like him, that he was a nice guy, we shot pool together. No way. Now that this has come out about this guy. Nobody liked him, everybody was afraid of him, what the hell do you think they are going to say?"

"I agree with you. I remember there was one lady in the box factory that worked with him. I remember her saying to me that one day she specifically asked him what he thought about the murders, and if he knew these people. And she said the weirdest thing: he just sat and stared at her for about 5 to 10 seconds. He then looked down on the ground and said to her, 'I don't know anything.'

"Yeah," Chubbs added, "Chief, I remember one day Tony and I we're interviewing some of the guys at his work who worked on the assembly line at the box shop. Tony, remember the guy who always wore that goofy hat and had his cigarettes rolled up in his sleeve? The guy was so ugly he could scare the devil himself. I asked this guy, I said to him. 'What kind of guy was this kid? Was he a tough guy, was he shy, or what?' 'He looked at me and said, 'No he's not a bad ass, he's what we call punk ass.' I thought to myself and I said too Tony on the way out to the car, if he is such a punk ass, he sure scared a hell of a lot of people."

"You know, Chubbs, you don't have to be a tough guy to scare a lot of people. From what you and Tony tell me, and from what I seen, he is a little guy, am I correct."

"You're correct, Chief, Chubbs and I both agree that he stands about 5'7", probably weighs only about 150 pounds, if that. Really he's not a bad looking guy. I mean he is not scary looking or ugly looking. Thick black hair, no facial hair, no tattoos. He doesn't dress flashy, I mean he's not real stylish. And when we interviewed him, he spoke real soft. I'll be honest with you, Frank, I do have my doubts, and often in our interviews he kept asking about his mother. He wanted to know how she was doing. He kept telling me when he's talking to me about his mother that he wanted the people to leave her alone. That she did nothing to them, that they were driving her crazy, they were making her mad. In his eyes his mother was all he had. He didn't want anybody to hurt her or anything to happen to her. Now, could she have been going through her change of life... possibly. Could the change of life thing make her go off the deep end... possibly. Anyway you look at it, Frank, five people are dead. Another family believes in a superstitious curse, and almost a whole town was in complete fear of a killer. That's about all I can say... We're trying to do our best. If we find out more information, you will be one of the first to know, okay?"

"Okay, guys, I got a meeting I have to be at in a half an hour with the mayor. I believe you guys are doing a good job. Stay on this as long as you can or until something else comes along and I got to pull you off. Try talking to as many people you can in town. Right now, what you're going to hear is either some more bullshit, some more fabrication, or maybe some truth."

"Frank, one last thing. If it's okay with you, we'd like to interview the psychiatrist that this guy Volpe talked with. You know the one he wanted to exorcise the evil spirits from the seven people on the list he had."

"Yeah, Tony, I think it's a good idea. I think you and Chubbs are making some good headway with that."

"Frank, one other thing: Chubbs and I want to thank you for all your help and support on this case."

"You're welcome. Listen to me, I like you guys, and I really do think you're doing a good job. Hang in there."

"Oh, Chubbs I meant to ask you, are you gaining a little bit of weight?"

"I don't think so, Chief...why?"

"Because if your ass gets any bigger, you're going to have to shit in the bathtub. Ha ha ha ha ha........"

"Thanks, Chief, I feel a lot better now."

"Come on, Chubbs, it's amongst friends. I love you like a son, now be safe out there both of you."

Lupo and Chubbs left the chief's office. Walking down the stairs to their office, Chubbs turned to Lupo and said, "You know I like the chief ,but he could be a real pain in my ass."

"Yeah, I know what you mean and you got enough ass for him to be a pain in. Ha ha ha ha," Tony chuckled.

"Oh good, thanks, Tony, now you got to be a funny guy. Ten Thousand comedians are out of work, and you and the chief crack jokes."

"You know I love you, Chubbs, like a brother. Come on let's go get lunch,... my treat."

8 DeSeco Family Reunion

t was 9 o'clock on Saturday morning and the Lupo family was getting ready for the DeSeco family reunion. This reunion is from Tony's mother Vivian's side of the family. They have this family reunion almost every year or at least every other year. This year the reunion was being held at Green Lane Park. The park offered outdoor recreation: swimming in the Perkiomen Creek, boating, fishing and a very nice setting of picnic tables with two covered pavillions that could accommodate up to 100 people. The Lupo and the DeSeco families look forward to the reunion because they always have a good time, especially Tony. He enjoys the family reunions. No matter whether it's from his mother's side or his father's side of the family, he enjoys having a good time. His only concern, as he mentioned to his wife Cathy as they were leaving the house, was that he didn't want to talk to anyone about the "Evil Eye" murders. He was hoping that the conversation about the murders or the person convicted of the murders would not come up at any time. Although, in reality he knew someone would bring up something about the "Evil Eye Murder Case." He also was aware that he would deal with it the best way he could and just try and make the information about the case short and to the point, and to inform his relatives that he really could not comment on the case. Anything he could tell them would be pretty much along the lines of whatever they read in the newspaper.

Tony always enjoys talking to his aunts, his uncles, and mostly enjoys talking to his cousins. The DeSeco family reunion can get as large as

50 people. Tony will see his Uncle Antonio DeSeco, his Uncle Johnny DeSeco, and his Aunt Josephine. Tony's cousins we'll be there for sure. Tony, as well as his cousins, look forward to seeing each other. He especially enjoys talking to his cousin Vinnie. Tony and Vinnie are close in age and enjoying laughing and joking about the family. Vinnie, who is around six feet tall, thinly built, and has thinning hair, always wears his black rimmed glasses. He is the kind of guy that always has something funny to say about people in the family, people he works with, or just people in general. He's always making a wisecrack. He is always cursing when he's talking about something. He also uses a good bit of Italian curse words or slang words when he's talking about something or somebody. If there is someone he's making fun of, he will call them a *jabroni* in Italian which means a loser or moron in English. **Gabbadost** means hardhead, and **ghiacchieron** means blabbermouth. He also uses the word *minchia* in Italian which means cock in English. This type of vocabulary is basically homegrown from the North Oak and Green Hill area. To this day Anthony Lupo only knows of these words from his hometown because of what his family and friends say that the slang words mean in English. With this family reunion there will be laughing, mocking each other, playing jokes on one another, and plenty of food, such as hotdogs, hamburgers, hot and sweet Italian sausage, Aunt Marie's homemade surfreet, roasted peppers, and various types of olives and cheeses. Everyone from the family brings food and also they chip in for some beer. Of course, there is some good homemade Italian wine. Some of the family members will bring homemade potato salad, coleslaw, pickled beets, and various types of fresh fruit from their gardens. The biggest treat for everyone in the family is always the dessert tray. If the desserts we're not homemade, like Aunt Vivian's chocolate cake or Aunt Marie's homemade apple pie, then there always is fresh made cannolis or pizzelles from Schettone's market. Schettone's market was one of the favorite Italian delis in the North Oak area. You could always get great Italian food from Schettone's. They make the best hot and sweet Italian sausage in the area and have a good assortment of olives, pickles, vegetables, cold cuts, and, of course, a great bakery department.

When all the family members arrive and everybody's done hugging, kissing, and laughing with each other, the women will start setting the

tables for the food by putting the plastic tablecloths on the wooden picnic tables and keeping one eye on the food and one eye on their children
who are playing and running around. The men will start teasing each
other and joking with one another. Some will start drinking and some
will start smoking. While all the laughing, talking, and joking is going
on, the older female cousins are helping their mothers set the table and
talking to their other female cousins about where they purchased their
new Bermuda shorts and the new blouses they're wearing. They also are
talking about the new boyfriends they have and who is on the cheer-
leading team and which teacher is a pain in the neck in school.

Tony was talking to some of his uncles that he hadn't seen for a while.
They were laughing and joking and talking to Tony about their aches
and pains. It was just about that time that his cousin Vinnie called them
over to where he was sitting with two of Tony's other cousins, Ralphie
and Joey, who are brothers from the DeSeco side of the family. Ralph
is in the real estate business and is doing very well for himself. He's a
short stocky guy with straight black hair pushed straight back on top of
his head. Joey is a supervisor at one of the local Italian market chains.
He is not married, in his late 30's, and still lives with his parents. One
of Joey's favorite pastimes is gambling whether it be horseracing at the
local track, playing pool at Sal's pool hall, or playing cards at one of
the Italian American Club in North Oak. When Tony was done talking
with his uncles, he excused himself and told them that he would be back
because he wanted to see what his cousin Vinnie was up to. He told his
uncles jokingly, "I hope I don't have to see someone about a traffic ticket, if you know what I mean." His uncles started to laugh. As Tony was
walking over to see his cousin Vinnie, his Uncle Antonio shouted over
to Tony, "If Vinnie gives you a hard time, Tony. Lock his ass up and
throw away the key."

As Tony was walking over to talk with his cousins, he thought to himself, *I hope I don't have to get Vinnie or any of my other cousins out of any
type of a jam because my card for getting out of jail free is not working today.*

Before Tony got over to his cousins, his wife Cathy walked up next to
him, leaned over and asked him if anyone in the family had mentioned
anything that had to do with the "Evil Eye Murder Case." Tony put his

arm around his wife, held her close to him, and whispered in her ear as he planted a kiss on her cheek, reassuring her that so far there was no talk from anyone about anything to do with the case. He told her, "So far, so good, not to worry. I have everything under control."

"Hey, Tony, was Uncle Antonio telling you about all his aches and pains or maybe about his latest hemorrhoid operation?"

" Vinnie, come on now, give Uncle Antonio a break, you know he's got more aches and pains than Carter has liver pills. It's good to see you Vinnie, Ralphie, and Joey. How you guys doing? If I know Vinnie, he's probably telling you some crazy joke, right?"

"Actually, Tony, what I was starting to tell Ralphie and Joey was about this guy that I work with at DeNero's food store. He says to me one day, 'Hey, Vinnie, how come you always say that word *Minchia*. What does it mean?' Well, you guys know it means prick in Italian, but this guy he doesn't know what it means, and a couple of my other Italian buddies and me—we were on break drinking coffee—they know what it means, right. So I said to this guy, *Minchia* means you're a nice guy. Now, if somebody says to you you are a *testa di minchia* that means you are a good guy. Now if someone says to you you are a *minchiata,* well, then you are the best guy ever to them. You are special to that person."

Right after Vinnie said that all of his cousins just started to laugh and shake their heads, telling Vinnie he's a crazy bastard.

"Hey, I'm telling you guys, as I am saying this to this guy, we all were laughing our asses off. I had them guys crying, they were laughing so hard. The guy that I was telling this to is a nice guy; his name is Mike Smith. I didn't have the heart to let him believe that, so later on that day I told him that *Minchia* meant cock in Italian and that it was a North Oak thing. He said to me, 'You mean that it originated in North Oak, or do they say that slang word in Italy?' So I say to him, 'You know something, Mike, I think we invented it in North Oak.' Then I said to him, 'A cock is a cock no matter how you say it, but you're not a cock. You're a really a nice guy.' He started to laugh, looked at me, and said, 'Vinnie, you always get me, but you are a good guy.'

After Vinnie got done telling his story and all his cousins started to joke and laugh with one another, their Aunt Marie told everyone it was time to sit down and eat. There must have been close to fifty family members at the DeSeco reunion; but before they started to eat, it was Uncle Johnny who stood up and told everyone to bow their heads and say grace. After everyone had finished saying grace, Uncle Antonio and Uncle Johnny and Aunt Josephine all held up a glass of homemade Italian wine and said to everyone, "*salud chindon*" which means good health for a hundred years. After the family was done drinking and eating, it was time for the desserts to come out; there were various types of Italian treats that everyone enjoyed immensely. It was at that time that Tony's cousin Joseph leaned over and quietly asked Tony if there was any more information on the "evil eye murders" or the killer himself. Tony thought to himself, *I guess I was kidding myself if I thought no one in the family would bring it up about either the murders or the murderer.* He didn't want to really get in to a lengthy conversation or even discuss the case, but his cousin Joey was a standup guy, and Tony knew he was just curious as were a lot of other people. Tony looked over at his cousin Joey and said, "Law-enforcement believes that they have the right person."

"Listen, Tony, I know we're all here to have fun, and I don't like to bring anything up about work, especially at a time like this, but I just wanted to ask you a question. In your opinion, do you think it's really about an evil eye curse or loansharking, and did they catch the right person that was connected to the murders?"

"Okay, Joey, I got to be honest with you: I really can't talk about the case, and I'm sure you understand why. What I think is there are some things I tried to understand and there are other things that I probably will never understand. It seems to me that no matter where I go, whether it's with the family, friends, or other people I see on the street who know me from the newspaper articles they come up to me and ask me questions that I just can't answer."

"I understand, Tony, and there's no hard feelings. I know that you're probably aware of all the talk that's going on out on the street. You know people are always talking because this murder case is a big thing in our town; and no matter if I'm shooting pool over at Sal's pool hall or playing cards at the East End Italian American Club, the guys are always saying either it's a loansharking thing or that this guy Volpe did really kill them people. You know, people are going to talk about all kinds of bullshit. Some of these guys where I play cards know you're my cousin, and I don't know if they're just breaking my balls, but some of the things that they are saying may be true."

"You know something, Joey, you're right. Maybe they're just breaking your balls, feeding you some bullshit, or trying to give you a hard time because I'm your cousin or maybe some of it is true. It's a shame that this had a happen for all the families involved in this case. The only thing I can really tell you—and it's coming from my heart you are my cousin, we have a great family, and we are so lucky to be blessed with all these wonderful people. Whatever these guys are saying at Sal's pool hall or the East End Italian American Club, take it with a grain of salt because at the department, believe me, Joey, we hear all the same kind of stories about this case. Listen, we all know North Oak is a nice town. It's where some of us were born and raised, and we are raising our children here. There's not a lot of major crime in this town like there is in the city. When something like this happens, I'm sure it's a big thing. Five people were murdered. People are scared. This is how it becomes a big thing. There's going to be all kinds of speculation and theories as to why it happened, who did what, and so on. We at the police department don't like to hear about this. We don't like to deal with this type of crime, but it's something that happened. It doesn't happen every day, but we just deal with it ok. I deal with it the best way I can. I'll say it again: North Oak is a damn good town. In this town we have the Italian families, the Polish families, the Irish families, the Black families, all kind of families, and for the most part ,we all get along pretty well. We all do the best we can do. With that said, what do you say that you and I go over to the dessert table and get some homemade cannolis?"

The two cousins put one of their hands on top of the other cousin's shoulder, they looked at each othher, laughed together, and walked over to the dessert table.

9 The Psychiatrist

Lupo was driving Route 29 along the Schuylkill River. It was about nine in the morning and a nice day for a ride, especially along the river. The sun was bright and traffic was not so heavy; most people were already at work. It was a good day to take a ride. He was cruising along Route 29 enjoying the beautiful day on his way to see Doctor Stanley Freeman, the criminal psychiatrist that Detective Lupo had questioned before. He was also the psychiatrist to whom John Volpe presented the list of the seven people he wanted exorcised of evil spirits. Lupo wanted to see the doctor by himself, so he left Chubbs back at the office to go over some other aspects on the case. In reality, he did not know what to expect by talking to the doctor the second time around. It was clear that when he called the doctor for the second interview he had seemed a little bit standoffish. As he told Lupo on the phone, he did not know what more he could add to the case; the individual was already convicted of the murders. Lupo tried to reassure the doctor that he only needed a few minutes of his time.

It took him about 25 minutes to arrive at the doctor's office. The doctor's office was in an addition on the backside of a hugh estate which was located in the town of Glenville. Glenville is a nice town that sits out in the countryside about 10 to 15 miles outside of North Oak. To the local people in the area, Glenville is noted for Buck Mountain which is the local ski resort. The resort is about 30 to 35 miles northeast of Philadelphia. As Lupo pulled up to the doctor's office, he noticed that the six-foot black wrought iron gates were not open. He also noticed on each side of the gates where two stone pillars about seven to eight feet high, and at the top of the pillars was a gargoyle that stood about three feet high.

Lupo thought to himself, *This place is beautiful. I was thinking that it was going to be off a sidestreet possibly a little office in a row house. Boy, was I wrong. OK, Doctor this is a nice estate. Who could afford to come to see this guy? I wonder what his hourly rate would be.*

As Lupo pulled his car up to the gate, there was a sign attached that stated: You will be entering into a high security area. There are security cameras monitoring the estate twenty four hours a day seven days a week. Press the intercom button and someone will direct you.

Lupo rolled down his window and pressed the button. A voice coming from the intercom stated, "Announce who you are and state your business."

"Hello, my name is Detective Anthony Lupo. I have a 10 o'clock appointment with Doctor Stanley Freeman."

Again a voice from the intercom said, "Proceed straight ahead and park in the yellow parking area. When you exit your vehicle, proceed to the main lobby's front door. Press the intercom button and announce who you are. A medical assistant there will greet you. Please tell them you're here to see the physician in office number 324.

Lupo thought to himself, *"Doctor Freeman is really doing well for himself. It seems like the good doctor is moving up in the world. This place is a lot different than our first meeting."*

Lupo entered the building and was greeted buy a large man about six feet five, dressed in black slacks and in a white medical lab coat. The assistant showed Lupo to the room, opened the door, and informed him to have a seat. Doctor Freeman would be with him shortly. The assistant turned, opened the door, and left the room.

Tony sat in the room waiting for the doctor. He noticed certain pictures on the wall and the huge bay window behind his desk. He also noted the mahogany desk with the large black leather chair behind it. On the top of the doctor's desk was a small day calendar, a miniature brass canon, and a crystal glass holder for his pencils and pens. He also noticed on one section of the wall was a saying written by someone anonymous that read:

The human mind knows many things. The human mind cannot know everything. Some minds may know several things. Some minds may not know anything. The mind can be a fantastic thing. The mind can be a dangerous thing. In your mind, what kind of things do you know?

After reading the saying on the wall, Tony thought to himself, *I wonder what kind of mind Doctor Freeman has. Personally, I believe a lot of these shrinks could use a shrink.*

At that moment the large brown wooden door opened in the center of the wall, and Doctor Freeman entered the room.

"Good morning, Detective Lupo, I hope you have not been waiting long. How are you today?"

"Good morning, Doctor Freeman, I'm fine, and thank you for taking the time to see me. I have not been waiting long at all." Lupo stood up and extended his hand to greet the doctor, and the two men shook hands. Lupo was sizing up the doctor in his mind. The doctor was a large man about six feet two, stocky build with brown hair and a thick beard and mustache, a very distinguished looking gentleman he was wearing plastic black rim glasses, a white shirt, a brown and white bowtie, and a brown tweed sport coat.

"Okay, Detective, what can I do for you today?" he asked as he took a sip of his coffee.

"Several years ago there was a murder in my hometown that I was investigating. I know you may see several patients a day or week, but we had talked about maybe a year or a year and half ago about one particular patient. The patients name is John Volpe. To refresh your memory a little bit more, you and I had this conversation about this young man.

He came to you with a death list of seven people that he wanted to exorcise of evil spirits."

"Yes, yes, yes, Detective, I do remember Mr. Volpe and I do remember the case. He came in off the street at my office in North Oak. Now, if I'm correct, that's where you and I had our first meeting. I still have a satellite office in North Oak where I see some of the people from the local state hospital there. Through the years I have studied the behavior of the criminally insane, and belong to the research center there with a staff of twenty people. Now as I said before, I do remember Mr.Volpe, and I do remember him coming in to my office in North Oak . If I am correct, he was caught, captured, and sentenced if I'm not mistaken."

"Yes, you are correct, Doctor Freeman."

"If that is the case, what is it I can do for you?"

"I know you're very busy, and I do not want to take much of your time. I just really only have a couple of questions that maybe you can clear up for me."

"Thank you for your concern, Detective. You are correct I am extremely busy, so without further ado may we proceed so we can conclude our time together."

"I'm having some trouble, Doctor, trying to fully understand this case. You see when we talked before, meaning when I saw you before, it was under the circumstance of the five murders known as that time the 'Evil Eye Killings.' Now, through some of my research I have found that there was some type of criminal involvement with money and this evil eye superstition. Dating back to the 1950's, actually back to April 1950 to be exact. My first question to you, Doctor, is when Mr. Volpe came to you with this death list was there any mention of other people that he wanted to put on the list and was there any mention of people dating back to the 1950's?"

" No, he did not mention anything dating back that far or any other people on his list that I can recollect."

"My next question is, in your estimation would you say that Mr. Volpe was mentally insane, mentally deranged, had a great deal of anger, or was plain out one crazy person?"

"Yes, Detective, OKAY I see we are talking about chemically unbalanced, depression, criminally insane and so on. You see, there are many issues and many explanations in theories of mental growth or decrease in the brain. Examples are from various psychologists, psychiatrists, psychoanalysts. Let me take, for an example, someone whose knowledge and wisdom I have great respect for. Doctor Sigmund Freud. Freud emphasized the importance of the unconscious mind, and he believed that the unconscious mind governs behavior to a greater degree than people suspect. You see the goal of psychoanalysis is to make the unconscious, conscious. It is believed that some aspects of nerve cells in the brain communicate through chemicals called neurotransmitters. Imbalance of one or more neurotransmitters such as gaba, norinephrine or serotonin can cause anxiety or anxiety-like symptoms. Mental illness of such a severe nature is that a person cannot distinguish fantasy from reality. They cannot conduct their affairs due to psychosis and may be subject to uncontrollable impulsive behavior. Let me give you another example: Another individual that I found very interesting is a psychologist named G Stanley Hall who devoted a large amount of his work to understanding adolescent development, particularly in the area of aggression. His theory was that mental growth proceeds by evolutionary stages."

Detective Lupo spoke up and interrupted Doctor Freeman. He held out his right arm and asked the doctor to stop for minute. He felt that Doctor Freeman was giving way too much information on what he thought was a simple question.

"I am sorry, Doctor, for interrupting you, but I do believe, and I think we both believe, that Mr. Volpe had mental problems. I personally do not understand all the psychoanalysis information you've given me, but I'm sure you are correct in all that you say. I am only interested in that death list of seven people he gave you. I want to know if there were any more people either on the list he gave you or maybe other people he may have talked to you about that were not on that list."

"To be quite honest with you, Detective, he wasn't there at the time when he was at my North Oak office for an evaluation, and quite honestly, I did not try to evaluate him. He was there as you say with the list of people—seven to be exact— that he had told me he wanted to exorcise of evil spirits. That's it, plain and simple. Now, if you are asking me questions about his mental status,well, that's a question that should be brought up to our Board of Physician. They had the initial evaluation of Mr.Volpe. When a patient comes into our clinic here, I myself and other physicians have an initial evaluation of that individual. However, there is a process from beginning to end that our patients must go through, an evaluation process with various physicians and even further evaluations that are done by a Board of Physicians who would research and evaluate his condition, and then they would make the final judgment on the case. You see, Detective, at our clinic we deal with various types of mental disorders, not only the criminally insane. I was one of the physicians that evaluated Vincent Jones. I'm sure you remember him: he was the murderer on the Marianne Twitchell case. As you remember, she was the young lady that was brutally beaten, raped, and murdered in Stonebury. The Board of Physicians will take my evaluation of any individual into consideration. However, you must understand the Board of Physicians has the final say on insanity, clinically insane, criminally insane, and so forth. I hope I'm clear on this fact for you, Detective."

"Yes, Doctor, you're very clear on this ...but my question is, if he wasn't here for evaluation, he was here for a purpose; and if I'm correct, the purpose was for you or whoever to exorcise some type of ritual on the people that were on the list that he presented to you,... am I correct?"

"Yes, that is correct. But you must remember I did not do an evaluation on Mr.Volpe. Also I informed him that I could not help him, and I did not fully understand what he wanted. There were times he could be a little persistent, very persistent, if he did not like what I was telling him, and that's when I informed him that I'm not a **witch doctor.** I don't do this type of service, nor do we do this type of service at our clinic."

"What was his reaction when you informed him that you could not help him with his death list or exorcism list?"

"Obviously, he was not a happy man. He murmured something that this was a waste of his time and he was going to seek help from another avenue, if I can recollect correctly his tone and mannerisms. He then got up and walked out the door."

"Do you know, Doctor, if he came with anyone or how he got here?"

"As a matter of fact, when he left and he walked out of the room, I got up from my desk and I looked out my window, and I did notice someone in a car pull up next to him on the street. It looks to me as though the person in the car may have been another man because I did notice the person in the car was wearing a hat. He and the young man were having some type of conversation. Then the young man waved his arm to the person in the car as a motion for him to go away. After the car pulled away, the young man proceeded to walk down the sidewalk until I could no longer see him. I am sorry, but I could not tell you what the person driving the car looked like."

"So, what you're telling me is that there was a man in a car talking to Mr. Volpe, correct?"

"Yes, Detective, that is correct."

"Well, Doctor, now I am curious. When I interviewed you the last time you did not mention another person.... why?"

"I believe the reason is simple...you did not ask me. If I recollect and my memory serves me right, you were more interested in the list he had of the seven people. If you remember and if my memory serves me right again, we talked about the possibility that there could have been a professional hit on these people. We also discussed that there could have been a long simmering feud between the families that may have finally come to a head. And if I might add—and I do not want to complicate any type of investigation— Mr. Volpe may have committed a murder or some of the murders but not all of the murders."

"My thoughts exactly. I am glad you brought that up. I have thought about that possibility myself. Let me ask you, could you tell if the person in the car could have been a younger or older gentleman, maybe some one he knew? I need too ask you again. Did he mention anything about his father or his mother?"

"As I remember, he did mention his father maybe once or twice, but he was very concerned and mentioned several times about his mother. He would say that they, who ever they are, would not leave her alone. That those people would always bother her and his family."

"Doctor, I have one last question. In your years of practice with the criminally insane or just emotionally disturbed, does this type of person act alone? Do they do their own planning? Or could there be an adult, a father, mother, or any type of person educating them or coaching them on how to do a violent act such as murder? The reason I'm asking you this is because someone once said to me, 'Most children will do what they are told as long as someone tells them what to do.' I know Mr. Volpe is not a child, but a man who is not in his right mind and may listen to someone such as a parent.... would I be correct on this?"

"I don't know where you're going with that question, Detective, but the statement you just said could be true. I will tell you this: I have always been under the assumption that when a man does not know what he's doing, then he really does not know himself. Look into your own questions, Detective, you may find your answer. It could be in the questions you asked yourself and you just asked me. May I say that the human mind is a very complex thing. Whether it is good or evil, the wheels in the mind keeps spinning and spinning until it stops forward or onword. When it starts to spin in reverse, then, that, Detective, in my estimation is when you have a problem. Let me bring your attention to one another thought. In my understanding with my patients and somewhat in this case, this type of superstition can lead to a number of uncomfortable feelings or situations. I have known some cases that I have spoken of with my colleagues in the medical field who tell me that some people believe they're sick and actually would go to an emergency room and complain of sickness brought on by an evil spell. The point that I'm trying to make is to give you some type of mental comfort, if I may use that term. Talk to someone in the medical profession, and you may get a better idea of how... or why... this type of murder took place. Just a little idea I have for you to think about. I personally don't know if it will help you in your case, but it may help you to try and understand this type of case or this type of superstition."

"Okay, Doctor, thank you for that thought, I may just take you up on that."

"Now I am sorry, Detective, but I have a meeting to attend. I hope I have been some help to you. I know you have some more questions that I hope you get the correct answer to. As for now, have a good day."

"I thank you once again for taking your time out of a busy day to see me. I'd also like to apologize for my outburst last time we met: The theory you had about fear and superstition that can complicate us to relinquish the common in favor of the bizarre. That both of us could murder somebody. It did upset me, and I'm sorry I walked out on you. I am just a common man that thinks in simple ways. I may not agree with the thinking of a psychiatrist or the understanding of psychology, but I do try and understand. I came here to talk about a perpetrator in a murder case and not to undergo any type a psychoanalysis. I will try and remember to keep in mind the theories of psychology and to understand your eval-uations. With that being said, Doctor Freeman, have a good day."

Lupo and the doctor stood up together. Detective Lupo leaned across the desk and shook Doctor Freeman's hand. As Lupo was leaving the clinic and walking to his car, he was thinking to himself and wondering who was the person who stopped their car and tried to talked with John Volpe that day when he went to visit Doctor Freeman. He thought to himself, *Could that have been one of his parents? Maybe a person that John Volpe did not like or maybe a friend? It could not be a friend. John Volpe was a loner, he really didn't have many or any friends at all. He had his family and that was all.*

10 Doctor Fitzgibbons

A s he was driving back to the police station after his meeting with Doctor Freeman, Lupo was thinking that maybe a medical doctor may have some good input for him on this type of evil eye sickness . He wanted to talk to a doctor from the medical profession to see if in fact there have been some reports of people complaining about sickness or pain stemming from some type of superstition, not necessarily the evil eye superstition but some type of superstition that could bring on this kind of sickness.

Luckily, the very next day Lupo had set up an appointment to talk to Doctor Gerald Fitzgibbons who worked in the emergency room at Saint Stephen's hospital on the Main Line, about 10 miles outside the city of Philadelphia. He had gotten this lead to talk to Doctor Fitzgibbons from his brother Salvatore who had informed him that Doctor Fitzgibbons was a graduate from Yale and had a special interest in the studies of ancient mythology and medicine dealing with various types of beliefs that are widespread on every continent. Some of the areas that he studied were the Middle East, Asia, Central America, and so on. He also studied the beliefs in medicine from countries such as Greece and Italy. Sal had become acquainted with Doctor Fitzgibbons at the University of Pennsylvania. Both Salvatore Lupo and Doctor Fitzgibbons had studied at the University of Pennsylvania's Medical School. Lupo had set up a meeting with Doctor Fitzgibbons the very next day at the doctor's office next to the University of Pennsylvania Hospital. Doctor Fitzgibbons was more than happy to meet with Detective Lupo because of his relationship with his brother, Sal.

Lupo arrived at the hospital at approximately 10 AM for his 10:15 appointment. When he arrived at the hospital, he was directed to go to the second floor to the west side of the building, room 32. Lupo took the elevator from the ground floor to the second floor, got off at the second-floor, walked to his right about 20 feet, opened the door, and was greeted by a very attractive young lady who happened to be Doctor Fitzgibbon's secretary. Lupo introduced himself and the secretary asked him to have a seat. "Would you like a cup of coffee? Doctor Fitzgibbons will be with you in a minute." Lupo declined the coffee and waited comfortably for the doctor. It was only about a minute and a half that Lupo had been waiting when the doctor came out of his office and walked up to Tony.

"Detective Lupo, how are you? It's so nice to meet you. I am Gerald Fitzgibbons. Come into my office and we can talk."

"Thank you, Doctor. Please call me Tony. It is pleasure meeting you. My brother has spoken so highly of you. Thank you for giving me your time."

"Fine, Tony, please call me Gerald."

The two men shook hands; and as they were walking into the physicians office, Doctor Fitzgibbons asked Lisa, his secretary, to hold all calls until after his meeting. At that moment both Tony and Doctor Fitzgibbons walked into his office and closed the door. As the two men entered the room, Doctor Fitzgibbons asked Tony to have a seat as he walked around his desk and sat down in his large black leather chair. Doctor Fitzgibbon's office was centered on the west side of the hospital which was known as Penn Medicine. The office overlooked Spruce Street in West Philadelphia.There was a large bay window behind the doctor's chair. The doctor sat behind a large cherry wood desk. On the walls of his office hung diplomas and plaques of the doctor's achievements and studies that he had completed. Lupo noticed on the right side behind the desk next to the window was a three-foot bronze statue of a gentleman wearing a physicians coat, a pair of wire rim glasses, and a stethoscope. On the left side behind the doctor's desk next to the window stood a two-foot high statue of an elephant made of white china with gold trim. Also on both sides of the office walls were paintings, sketches, and prints of very famous artists. He also noticed pictures of famous people and physicians. On the right wall was a picture of Doctor Sigmund Freud and under the picture was written **Sigmund Freud a doctor of Neurology. The founder of Psychoanalysis and a doctorate in Neuropathology.** On the left side of the wall hung a picture of Hermann Hesse with a caption that said, **Herman Karl Hesse, German born poet, novelist, and painter.** And to the far right side of the picture of Hermann Hesse was a picture of Albert Einstein with one of his quotations beneath the picture that stated, **Imagination is more important than knowledge.** As Tony was looking around the room he thought to himself, *I think this Doctor Fitzgibbons is doing very well for himself and must be a very important man at the hospital. I would imagine that this guy's a real brainiac. I bet he has enough brains for three maybe even four people.*

"So, Tony, I could recognize you in a group of people that you are definitely Salvatore's brother. There is definitely a family resemblance. By the way, how is my old chum, Salvatore doing?"

"He is doing very well. Thanks for asking. He did tell me one thing that I should tell you. He said, 'Checkmate'."

Gerald laughed,"Yes, your brother and I played many and many a game of chess. And I might add that your brother is an excellent chess player."

"Well, Doctor, I mean Gerald, Sal said exactly the same thing about you."

"Listen, Tony, let's not be so formal. I will call you Tony. We can call him Sal. And you can call me Gerald or Jerry, okay?"

"Fine. That is good with me".

"Now, what can I do for you? When we spoke on the phone you mentioned something about superstitions and sickness. Am I on the right track, and did I understand you correctly?"

" You are correct. There's a murder case that I've been working on for quite a while. The case involves murder and superstitious beliefs, mostly from the Italian community of North Oak.

"I know it well. I have an aunt— my father's sister to be exact— who lives in West Conshohocken, so I know exactly where you're talking about. Excuse me, I'm sorry for the interruption. Please continue."

"As I was saying, the individual involved with the murders has been arrested. Through further examination of this case, I am trying to figure out if there could have been anymore suspects, but mostly I'm trying to understand the why and how of this case. During my investigation I had an interview with a Doctor Freeman, a criminal psychiatrist, who interviewed the individual who committed the murders. At the time that I spoke to this doctor, he informed me that there are people who actually believe in a superstition that can make them physically and mentally sick. Now, with my lack of experience in this field, I spoke to my brother Sal, and he informed me that it is true some people can in fact make themselves feel physically or mentally sick. My brother then informed me that you would be the best person for me to talk to about the subject."

" I find this very interesting. I might add that your brother is a very good physician in his own right, and I thank him for his compliment. Now, with that being said, I strongly do agree with him. Let me talk to you first of all about superstition, the belief in superstition, and sickness. In my studies throughout the world, I have found that if a person wants to believe in this or that type of superstition, then naturally they become superstitious, and by that I mean they become afraid for themselves and most of all what will happen to them. By becoming superstitious, you can then make yourself sick. I believe that the sickness, mental or physical, is not brought on by any type of superstition, it is brought on by the individual himself."

"Doctor, this is only my belief that the mystery behind any type of superstition may be stronger than trying to understand the type of superstition it is. Am I making any sense at all, or am I just rambling on, and please forgive me if I am?"

"No, Tony, you're not rambling on. It is a complicated subject. To some people it is very simple and to other people it's almost comical. Let me give you an example of what I mean: I actually experienced this first hand myself. I had been studying and working in Europe for about a year or more, and it was at that time that I worked in the emergency room of a hospital in the town of Agrigento, Italy. That is located near Sicily. A middle-aged, somewhat attractive lady came into the emergency room and was complaining of a sickness she said she had. She was complaining about headaches and her body hurt. She said she was afraid. I asked her what happened to her. She said to me, 'La Fatura'. At that time I did not know what La Fatura meant. All she kept saying was, 'La Fatura, La Fatura'. One of the nurses who was working with me in the emergency room told me that lady was saying 'La Fatura' and it it ment the Overlooks, Bad Eye, or Malocchio. As I was conversing with the nurse, she was informing me that the lady was complaining that someone had put a curse on her. They put an evil spell on her. It was at that very moment that the lady started to cry. She wanted to feel better. This went on for some time. There was another nurse working there who talked to her. She held her hand, and they were conversing in Italian: and while they were conversing, the other nurse pulled the curtains around the bed and went into support the young lady who was sick. It took about a half hour to forty minutes for all this type of procedure to be completed. After the nurse and the patient we're done talking, she thanked them and told them she felt a lot better and she wanted to go home. I had a chance to talk to the nurse who started the conversation with the young lady, and she informed me about the tradition that some people believe called 'La Fatura.' She explained to me that for centuries and to that day some of the Southern Italians, notably the older Sicilians, believed in that type of superstition, curse, or spell that this individual believed someone had put on her. It was then, Tony, that I realized how such a superstitious belief could impact an individual's health."

"Did you ever find out who put the curse on her and why?"

"No, we did not. I believe, if my memory serves me correctly, we were just concerned about making her feel better. And her main concern was to get better. I might add that superstitions can come in many forms. They can come from all types of people. And they can come from all parts of the world. In my understanding, it is what the individual believes in and what the individual understands. Do I have any better answer for you on this type of sickness. I'd have to say,... no. Do I see it every day? Again, I have to say no. It's just the way things are in certain societies. This type of belief or superstitions have been going on for centueries. I do not know of anyone that I have met in my profession that knows of any type of medical cure. I mean there is no pill or medication given to stop this type of belief or curse. Also, I might add this type of belief and superstition may continue to go on for years and centuries. It all depends the type of people and the type of environment that they are living in. You know, Tony, I will tell you one thing that seems to always fascinate me about these types of superstitions, or for that matter any type of superstition: It is not just poor people or people who are not well or people from certain countries or certain parts of the world that believe in some type of superstition or fear a certain type of superstition. It is a well-known fact that wealthy people, famous people, people from all walks of life would believe in such a thing. If you look up superstition in the dictionary and find the correct meaning of what that word means, it is simply this: It is a widely held but unjustified causation leading to certain consequences of an action or event, or a practice based on such a belief, and to further explain by this type of belief they're talking about a myth, old wives tales, legend or story and so on. So you see, Tony, the simple fact is there is no pill, no drug, no needle to correct someone's superstitious beliefs.

"I know what you'r saying, Jerry. I have almost a whole section of town that may believe in this curse. Some of the people, no excuse me, a lot of the people would not talk to us when we were investigating this murder case. So I am well aware of what you're telling me. I believe I have taken a good deal of your time. Thank you for enlightening me on some of the issues that I was not aware of. Thank you again for your time. It was a pleasure meeting you."

"It was my pleasure as well. I wish you well in your investigation, and please give my regards to your wonderful brother. I was an only child and Salvatore was like a brother to me. He is one of my very dearest friends. Please tell him that he did 'Checkmate' and won the game."

The two men stood up and shook hands and said their goodbyes. As Lupo was walking from the doctor's office, he couldn't help but think how kind and informative the doctor was.

11 A Mellow Time

T hings back at the office we're getting a little crazy. It seemed like Lupo was spending a lot of time researching the Evil Eye Case from 1950. At home there were times when the tension was building up between Tony and his wife. Tony and Cathy were bickering with each other. Cathy's way of thinking was that Tony was spending way too much time at the office. With three children, and one a baby over a year old, she would like Tony to spend more time with her and the family. The way Tony looked at it was he did spend as much time as he could give to her and the children. He did try to afford her the time she needed for herself. He tried to reassure her with reoccurring statements of the love that he has for her. At the office there was also some tension between Lupo and Chubbs. It wasn't a big deal. It was just everyday work that they may have been paying too much attention to.

It was time to take a break. Tony knew he had some vacation time on the books that he could use. He told Frank and Chubbs that he wanted to take a few days off. To get away and re-charge his battery. He had set things up with his brother and his parents to watch the kids for a day or two. They agreed. They knew that Tony was under some pressure and putting himself and his family through some strain. It seemed that Cathy talked to the family and mentioned to them that Tony and she would like some time to themselves. Cathy and Tony talked about it and agreed it would be good for them to take a couple days during the week to get away.

They headed up to their local favorite spot, Lancaster, Pennsylvania, or as some of the local people from the North Oak area would call it, "The Dutch Country." Lancaster is one of the birthplaces of the Pennsylvania Dutch and home to the Amish. It has beautiful farmlands, fresh produce, rolling hills, beautiful green grass. The Lancaster countryside is so pristine with beautiful country stores, beautiful huge barns and silos, many corn fields and wheat fields that surround Mother Nature's earth. Throughout the landscape you notice various types of farm animals, such as horses, cows, pigs, and sheep. You will see the men plowing the fields. You'll see the Amish women hanging their clothes out to dry in the fresh sunlight. You will see the children playing in their yards. Some of the children will be helping their parents working at the roadside stands selling flowers, produce, bakery goods, and the best apple cider around. One of the biggest thrills is to notice the horse and buggies that ride through the streets of Lancaster. There were fresh foods homemade pies, very friendly people, and so much more. It was about an hour's drive to the country side.

Lancaster was not that far away, but for both Cathy and Tony it seemed like it was in another world. It was their getaway, to get a way, to be with one another, and only for each other.

Cathy and Tony pulled out of their driveway and headed down the road when the conversation started as to which route they should take. Should they go the way of Route 23 which would be all the side roads and a little bit more scenic, or should they take 276, commonly known as the Pennsylvania Turnpike which is a much faster ride to their destination.

"Well, Cath, what do you want to do, turnpike or the back way?"

" It doesn't matter to me. Whatever you feel like doing is okay with me as long as we get there safe and sound."

"Let's take Route 23. It's a nice day for a ride. We'll take our time. We'll stop along the way before we get to Lancaster. Maybe we can pick up some fresh fruit and vegetables. We're staying at the bed-and-breakfast, right?"

"Yeah, but we could stop on the way back. It'll be good that way. I told the kids we would bring them some candy apples, and you know they went for that."

"You know, that's what I love about you, you're so easy to get along with, and you think of other people before yourself. We have a great family. I know we're going to have a good couple of days. It just feels good to get away, and I got to agree with you: You were right, this is what I needed. To me it is like another world up there."

"It is a lot different than the world you work in."

"You know I need to get my horseradish from Long's shop at the Lancaster Central Market, and we got to stock up on some other goodies at Stoltzfus. If I know you, I'm sure you brought the cooler so we can take it back home full of goodies."

"I did and don't let me forget the hot dogs and sausage. Anthony likes their sausage so we got to bring something back for the kids besides candy apples. Maybe we can get Jen an Amish doll for her dollhouse."

"You know something, Cathy, I enjoy this drive up to the Dutch country. It makes me feel good inside. It makes me fully understand how much we have. Not so much what we have, but what I have. First of all, we are truly blessed with wounderful kids. God is good to us and life is great. Maybe I don't say it often enough, and I'm sorry, but you and the kids are the best thing that ever happened to me."

"I want you to know that we love you very much and you're a good husband and a great father. Your life and your work is so much different from ours, and I try to understand how you do it. There's times I ask myself how you deal with violence, with murder. I know one thing, Tony, I couldn't do it, and that's why I believe that God puts people on this earth for special reasons. You're very special to me and our family, but I know deep in my heart you're a special detective. You really care about what you do."

"I'll tell you something, Cathy, and I'm not trying to feel sorry for myself, but you're right. Sometimes I feel that the world I work in is a world so different, actually completely different from your world. The world I work in is a world where it all happens. Where there is robbery, fighting, murders either from jealousy, money or something as crazy as an evil eye curse. A world of destruction, hate, misery and death. I myself do believe that some people are not a product of their environment...they make their environment."

Cathy and Tony stayed at a bed-and-breakfast called the Red Carrot. It was in the small town of Blue Ball in Lancaster County. They had stayed there before. It was one of there favorite places, and they knew the owners very well. Anytime they go to Lancaster, they always stay at the Red Carrot. This bed-and-breakfast is very clean; the rooms are clean, they have their own private baths, and the food is very good. The owners of the bed-and-breakfast where two older people of Dutch-German descent known as Emual and Sarah Kracks. Needless to say, Emual and Sarah enjoyed two of their favorite guests. The bed-and-breakfast is a three story old Victorian house built in 1856. This house had been in the Kracks family for a number of years. Emaul and Sarah are third-generation owners of the bed-and-breakfast. The house and the area around the house, including the front yard and the front porch, look like something taken from a Norman Rockwell painting.

When Tony and Cathy arrived at the Red Carrot, they were warmly and happily greeted by both Emaul and Sarah. As Tony and Cathy walked into the foyer of the beautiful Victorian house, Emaul with his broken English accent hollered out, "Anthony, it is good to see you, my friend."

Both Emaul and Sarah came into the vestibule to hug and greet their favorite guests. Emaul is a large man in stature: He stands about 6 feet three inches and has thick, wavy salt and pepper hair combed back on his head. He sports wire-rimmed glasses and a thick gray mustache. He wears suspenders to hold his pants up and has a jolly laugh. You would believe it was Santa Claus. Sarah, on the other hand, is a short busty lady. She is about five foot four and her silver hair is pulled back tightly in a bun. She also wears wire-rimmed glasses. They are two very happy and jolly people. Sarah is the type of lady that when she sees her friends she laughs with joy and clasps her hands together, happy to see her old friends. Sarah and Emaul wanted to make their guests feel very welcome. They took their luggage and all four of them went on the elevator to the third floor and walked to the rooms in the back of the house. As they walked into their room, Sarah and Emaul had a special treat waiting for them. Sarah was well-informed. She knew Cathy enjoyed her chocolate truffles, and she had a box of truffles waiting for her on the bedroom dresser. Emaul was also aware of Tony's taste for good vintage wine, so he had a bottle of homemade wine that a friend of his from Blue Ball made especially for him. Cathy and Tony informed their host that they were very grateful for the gifts that they received and mentioned to Sarah an Emaul that they would be staying for a few days and wanted them to join Cathy and Tony for a dinner the next night at a place called the Lancaster Seafood House.

It was at that point Sarah spoke up and said to Cathy and Tony, "Seafood is good. There will be no more knockwurst for this guy," pointing her thumb towards Emual.

Tony said to Sarah, "What do you mean?"

At that moment both Sarah and Emaul began laughing. Sarah then turned to Emaul and said, "You tell them why you should not eat knockwurst."

Emual said to Tony and Cathy as he chuckled along with his thick German accent, "The other night Sarah made some homemade sauerkraut and knockwurst for dinner and I may have had...you know, a little too much. As we were lying in bed, Buffy, our cat, was on top of the blankets. I had some gas and I farted. I farted so loud that Buffy jumped straight up almost a foot in the air and landed on the floor. We started to laugh so hard that Sarah farted, and it was at that time that Buffy ran out of the room."

Everybody laughed loudly. Cathy and Tony we're looking at each other laughing hysterically. Tony turned to Sarah and Emaul and said, "You know, my friends, that is something I needed, a good laugh and that is probably one of the funniest things I've heard in a long time. You guys are great. God bless you. We love you."

"We will see you for dinner around 6:30 if that's okay with you folks, and I promise you no knockwurst."

The next few days and nights that Cathy and Tony spent in Lancaster we're just what the doctor ordered for both of them. They felt like two young lovers again, walking around the towns, going antique shopping, shopping for art, eating good pastries, taking a horse and buggy ride, and sightseeing as much as they could.

Their last night staying with their friends at the bed-and-breakfast was the passion night they needed. It was a cool crisp night with a full moon in the sky. As they were getting ready to relax for the evening in their king-size bed, Cathy walked over behined Tony and put her arms around his neck and whispered in his ear for him to pull the curtains aside so that the moonlight would be the only light that would shine in the darkened room. As Tony proceeded to draw the curtains aside, Cathy took off her robe and dropped it to the floor. She then began to take Tony's robe off and drop it to the floor. Standing behind him she wrapped her one leg around his waist and began licking on his ear. Tony turned around, picked Cathy up, walked her over to the gigantic bed as he was kissing and licking her face, and her ears, working his way down to her beautiful warm breast. Together they fell on top of the bed in passionate agonizing lust for each other. The beautiful moonlight was shining off of their naked bodies as they proceeded to push and touch, lick and touch, to moan and whisper to each other the sounds of sexual passion and pleasure. It was the night that sexual passion released their emotional energy that they both had for one another. All that Tony could think about was how good, how great this felt, how badly he needed his emotions to release in such a wonderful way. He felt as if his body was floating on air. Her skin was warm and moist. He held her close; he squeezed his fingers into her back feeling as though he could push her body inside of his. They made love, and when they were done, they held onto each other. Cathy's head lay gently on top of Tony's right shoulder as he gently rubbed his hands so very softly along her arms. Their passion and their excitement overwhelmed the feeling they have for one another. It encapsulated their souls. It made them aware of their togetherness and no feeling of emptiness. It was as though their bodies became shadows in the midnight sky. They made love again; and when they were done, they caressed each other. When they made love again, they knew that they made love for each other because of each other and only for one another. As their bodies lay motionless on the bed, the moonlight shined a silhouette as it reflected off the mirror on top of the dresser to their naked bodies on the bed. Two people lying in complete and utter relaxation and totally satisfied.

Tony fell asleep and was dreaming. It was a dream that woke him up out of a sound sleep. Although he tried not to think about the murder case, it was that exact dream that woke him up. It was a dream about the person convicted. His dream was about the interview with John Volpe and John Volpe's family, particularly his mother. He had a dream that it was a movie he was looking at and not the real murder case. A dream where he could not get up out of his chair and walk out of the movie theater.

It was about 2:30 in the morning when Tony sat up on the edge of the bed. He reached over to the red and black velvet chair that was next to the bed and grabbed his underwear and put them on. He walked over to the sliding glass doors that led to the balcony. He pulled a chair over in front of the sliding glass door, sat down on the chair with his body hunched over in a frontal position and his arms across his legs, and just looked out at the open moonlit night sky. He knew he didn't want to think about it, and he didn't want to let any thoughts of the "Evil Eye Murder Case" enter into his mind, especially now while he was on vacation and away from all the craziness, not only of the crime itself but of the investigations, the people, and all the questions that he felt were unanswered. He knew in his heart that now was not the time to think about this case, but he was so involved that he started to wonder and to question himself. Is this case something that he has control of or is this case controlling him.

It was at that very same moment when a soft voice from behind him spoke. "Tony, honey, are you okay? What's the matter?"

Cathy, his lovely wife, asked in her very soft, gentle voice as she laid both of her hands on top of his shoulders and started rubbing and massaging around his neck area.

Tony reached his right hand around the top of his neck and laid his hand on top of hers.

"I'm okay, Cath, I just couldn't sleep. I guess I was a little restless and didn't want to wake you up. So I just wanted to sit here for couple minutes and look out at this beautiful scenery. I'm sorry if I woke you up. Please... go back to bed... really I am okay."

"Tony, I know something is bothering you, and I'm here for you to talk to me about it. Listen, if I tell you what I think it is, will you at least give me the satisfaction so I know I'm right. Is it about the 'Evil Eye Murder Case'?"

"You do know me very well. Yes, you're right. It is about the case and I'm sorry that it's on my mind now, but this case has been on my mind a lot. I know we're on vacation, and I'm sorry. But when I think about something about the case, then I start to try and figure out maybe different angles or reasons why."

"Tony, I don't understand what you're trying to figure out. You caught the man, he's in prison, he confessed, what more do you want? You just can't keep beating yourself up like this. What is it that you think you're missing or what is it that you're trying to connect. I don't understand. You're a good cop and a wonderful person. I know that you did the best you could on this investigation, and I believe in my heart and soul that you gave it 100%.

"It's about the victims and the the murderer himself. Something inside of me is thinking we didn't get the right person. I know you're right. I did give it 100%, and I thank you with all my heart and soul for all the love and understanding that you've given me. I'm glad you're in my life. You always have a way of making me feel better. Maybe you are right: Maybe I am thinking too much about this case, so for now, I love you and thank you for just being there for me. I may not tell you all the time how much I need you and I love you. You are the best thing that ever happened to me. Now, all I want to do is go to bed with my wonderful wife."

"That sounds good to me, honey. Let's just enjoy our time together."

It was 7:30 in the morning as the sunlight was shining in the room waking Cathy and Tony up as they were wiping the sleep from their eyes. Cathy leaned over and whispered in Tony's ear, "Let's take a shower together." While they were in the shower, they made love again and enjoyed each other one more romantic time. As they were packing their bags and getting ready to leave, there was talk between them about what to bring back for the kids. As they were checking out and getting ready to head home, Cathy and Tony said goodbye to Sarah and Emaul. They reassured their friends that they had a wonderful and enjoyable time and that they would see them again. Emaul shook Tony's hand and gave him a bear hug. Tony looked at Emaul and said to him, "It was great seeing you again, my old friend.You and Sarah are wonderful people. Thank you for being such a good friend today and always."

Emaul looked at Tony and said, "You are my friend today and today is now; tomorrow is the future and you will be my friend tomorrow and always. God bless you, Tony and Cathy; you both are beautiful people. Have a safe ride home."

12 Murder in King Of Prussia

It was 9:15 Monday morning and Tony was back in the office going over some old paperwork on the "Evil Eye Murder Case" Chubbs walked into the office and asked him how he enjoyed his time away in Lancaster County. Tony assured him it was an enjoyable few days, and as Tony explained to Chubbs it was the mental enema that he needed. They both got a laugh out of it, and Chubbs told Tony it was good to have him back. Tony asked Chubbs, "So how was last week? Where you busy?"

"Hell, yeah, I am so busy that instead of eight days a week, I need eight weeks in the day, if you know what I mean. I was busier than a one-legged man in an ass kicking contest."

"What's going on? Anything out of the ordinary or anything I should know about?"

"Yeah, there was a murder over in King Manor. Some guy killed a 12-year-old girl and now the investigators from King Manor and King of Prussia asked us for some input and if we knew the killer."

" Do we know who it is? Did they catch the person who killed the girl?"

"Yeah, they got him and I think that the Chief will probably talk to you about it today."

No sooner had Chubbs finished saying that and the chief walked up to Lupo's desk.

"Good morning, fellas, how's it going today?"

"Good, Chief, how about you? "asked Tony."

"Tony, you got a minute. I want to see you in the office to talk over a few things. Chubbs, have we heard anything more on the Lisa Kelly murder from any of the investigators in the King of Prussia-King Manor station?"

"Nothing so far, Chief. I was just filling Tony in with some of the details."

"Good. I want you to go over and talk to Lieutenant Murray about a robbery at Dave's Auto Body Shop. I will fill Tony in with the rest of the details on the Kelly murder. Tony, let's go to my office for a bit."

As Tony and the chief walked to his office, the chief asked Tony if he enjoyed his vacation and if he had a good time. Tony told him it was good to get away for a while, and that he and Cathy enjoyed it very much. When he entered the chief's office, he told Tony to sit down and take a load off his mind. The chief began to tell Tony about the murder of the 12-year-old Kelly girl. "What they know so far is that the suspect they caught is a 26-year-old male named Vincent May from the West Falls Area. This guy is a known pedophile and has been in trouble with the law before." He informed Tony that the suspect lived in the area. He said, "Just another sick son-of-abitch who just wasted a young child's innocent life." Lupo asked the chief if this was another gruesome murder along the lines of the Carri Anne Twitchell murder. Detective Lupo was thinking to himself, *If this is a gruesome murder, I just might want to be taken off the case.* Detective Lupo's thinking was that he was dealing with the evil eye murders which was taking up a good bit of his time. Lupo knew if he told the chief about how much of his involvement was invested in the case that the chief may take him off that case and direct him strictly to the Kelly murder. So Detective Lupo asked the chief questions pertaining to the Kelly murder. "Excuse me, Chief, let me ask you a question if I can?"

"Sure, go ahead, Tony, remember it's Frank, not Chief."

"Yeah, okay Frank... this Kelly murder, it's not as gruesome as the Carrie Anne Twitchell murder, is it? I mean, I know she was shot, but was there any other activity on the body if you know what I'm trying to say?"

"Yeah, Tony, I know what you're going say or what you're thinking. No the girl was not raped and there was no form of mutilation. It was one shot from a 12 gauge shotgun to her back. So far from what I understand, she was killed with a 12 gauge pump action Winchester Model 1912 shotgun. Apparently this guy was probably trying to have sex with her and to have his way with her. He was probably trying to rape her; and from what we gather, she started to run out of the area where it happened, which by the way was at the quarry down by Henderson and Third Avenue in King Manor. So what we know so far is that as she was trying to run away, and he shot her in the back and killed her."

"So, what is it, Frank, that you want me do on this case?"

"There's a detective from King of Prussia name Sullivan, Tom Sullivan, who called over here and said that this guy, the suspect, this Vincent May had some issues over here in North Oak. Apparently he is running around town and going to the local school yards and flashing and fondling himself in front of some of the kids in the playground. I'd like for you and Chubbs to see what you can find out about this asshole and go see this Detective Sullivan and just put some light on the subject with this guy. Apparently that's all they're asking us: what we know, if anything, about this guy."

"OK, I'll get Chubbs, and we will get on it right away. I will see what I can find out if I am able talk to some folks at the King of Prussia office.

"That will be good, Tony. Just remember we'll try to help them as best we can. We need to communicate. What we don't need is a conference."

" I understand perfectly what you mean".

"Oh, one other thing, listen, it's about this evil eye murder. I want to talk to you about something."

Tony was afraid that the chief would take him off of the old case. He probably would tell him they had caught the guy so everything was over.

"Listen, Tony, about this evil eye case and about this person that we have incarcerated. I've been talking to some people around town and actually to the perp himself. Now, before we get into anything, I want you to know that I'm not trying to take over your case. I truly believe that you and Chubbs are doing a hell of a job. From what I'm hearing is that there is a lot more to this case besides the five murders."

"What are you hearing?"

"My concern is about John Volpe himself. I personally believe that he was somehow involved in the murders, but the thing that I question is did he do it alone? There are a lot of stories going around about this case, and I just want to make sure. And I think you want to make sure that we have the right person, or do we have the right people in connection with this case? So here's what I'm going to do. I want you to stay on that case. Keep me informed if there's anything new that we may have overlooked or do not know ourselves. I mean it, Tony, I want to know even if a mouse farts. I need to know about it....you got it?"

"I got it, Frank. I believe you and I are thinking along the same lines, not only about the case and the people who were murdered but about Volpe himself or should I say maybe other suspects. I'll be honest with you, this case has got me baffled. I want to get to the bottom of it once and for all. I'll find out as much as I can about this little girl Kelly who was murdered. I can handle this and the evil eye murders and hopefully come up with some type of resolution or some type of ending to the "Evil Eye Murder Case," if there is such a thing as an ending."

Detective Lupo felt some relief that not only did he himself believe there could've been more than one individual involved in the murder, he now had someone else with criminal knowledge believing there may have been more than one person involved. Lupo actually thought to himself, *At least I'm not crazy.* There were times that he thought he was just spinning his wheels round and round and round. Detective Lupo is a good, honest man, he will follow up on the Lisa Kelly murder, and he will talk to Detective Sullivan as soon as he can, so he can put his efforts back into the evil eye case.

13 Decetive Sullivan

L upo set up a meeting with Detective Tom Sullivan for 10:00 the next morning to talk about the Lisa Kelly murder. He had concerns about the meeting and about how much assistance he could be. He arrived at the King of Prussia police station about 9:50 in the morning. He was by himself, simply because Detective McFadden was working on the robbery at Dave's Auto that the chief had directed him to do. Detective Lupo parked his car in the back of the police station and started to walk up to the main entrance. The King of Prussia area at the Upper Merion police station, as it's known, sits up on a hill that overlooks part of the King of Prussia shopping mall. The King of Prussia area back in the 50s and early 60s had a lot of farmland, and orchards. The police station itself is only about four or five years old with new technology. Detective Lupo walked in on the first floor of the main level into a wide open atrium surrounded by metal and glass sliding doors. He was greeted by a man who was a police cadet sitting behind a four foot by ten foot red brick wall enclosed with bulletproof glass. The cadet greeted Detective Lupo as Lupo mentioned to him about his meeting with Detective Tom Sullivan. The cadet informed him that Detective Sullivan was waiting for him. He leaned over, pressed the button, and the door on the left side of the enclosure opened, and Lupo walked back to the second office on his left. As he was walking down the hall, he noticed how clean and pristine the building was, and he also noticed the beautiful murals of the King of Prussia-Upper Merion area that hung on the walls. He noticed the number of portraits from various police chiefs, police officers, detectives and patrolman that were hanging on the walls in the corridor. He also was touched by the section of the hallway that was dedicated to fallen police officers. The memorial to the fallen officers touched Lupo in a profound way. Tony arrived at Detective Sullivan's office and knocked twice on the door. A clear and strong voice on the other side of the door said, "Please come in."

The two men shook hands and Detective Sullivan told Lupo to have a seat. Detective Lupo was somewhat fascinated with Detective Sullivan's office. It was above the parking garage with a huge window behind his desk overlooking part of the King of Prussia skyline. Detective Sullivan offered Lupo a cup of coffee before they started. Lupo thanked him but declined. He said, "I've already had two cups and that is my limit for the day." Both men laughed.

"Thanks for coming over to talk to us about this case. The information we have so far is that this suspect knew the victim; apparently, they knew each other from the neighborhood. One of the other detectives is interrogating him now to try and find out how the two of them ended up together. What we know so far is that he drove her to the quarry that is down at Henderson and Third Avenue in the King Manor area. He admitted to us he was trying to have sex with her, and that she resisted his actions. She jumped out of the truck and started to run away, and that is when he shot her in the back with a shotgun. After he shot her, this sick sonofabitch stood over her and told to us that he masturbated. I will tell you, Detective, it was very, very hard for me to control my anger and that's the reason why my partner is interrogating him instead of me. Now, my chief informed me that you may be of some help in letting us know anything about the suspect. He also informed me that you are a good detective with background in criminal knowledge, and I want you to know that I appreciate it very much."

"Thank you. I will try and support you with whatever knowledge I may have or our department has on the suspect."

"That's good, Tony, I do appreciate your help."

The two men got along very well. It was back-and-forth, it was information, it was support, and it was knowledge. It's the kind of knowledge that inspires individuals. It's the kind of knowledge that you want your police department to have, and it's the type of knowledge that you learn, that you earn, and these two men have that special gift. The two men talked for close to an hour and a half. They discussed various aspects of the crime, the crime scene, the suspect, and naturally of the victim herself.

The two men are similar in age, although Detective Sullivan is just a few years younger than Lupo. The two men also have similarities in their family life. Both men are married, both men have children almost the same age, and both men were raised in the local area. Both were surprised to know that they played football, almost the same position with their high school football team, and they enjoyed the game immensely. Near the end of their conversation Tom Sullivan informed Tony Lupo that he has been a big help to his investigation and that he would inform his chief about their meeting. He did, however, mention to Tony something that surprised him. He asked Tony how he was doing on the investigation with the murderer on the evil eye murders. It was at that very moment when Tony Lupo became very curious.

"I am surprised you asked me about that investigation, Tom. Right now, between you and me, I'm still doing some investigation on my own. There are some things that I still have questions about."

"If you don't mind me asking, Tony, could it be about the murder victims or about the murderer himself?"

Lupo was surprised again. He was wondering how and why Tom was asking specifically about John Volpe, and why now. "Well to be honest with you, Tom, it's about both, but my curiosity has got me a little bit interested in the murderer himself."

"Tony, if it is about John Volpe, as you say it is, let me assure you that what we are talking about now stays in this office. Could it be that you're thinking it's about his motive, or was he the one and only stalker?"

"I am a bit surprised that you mention this. Yes, my interest lies with two things, to be quite honest with you. One is the motive. I am Italian and I know about the evil eye curse. I myself do not believe in it. I believe in God. I believe it was more about a money thing more so than a superstitious thing. And second, I have this funny notion that the killer for some strange reason did not act alone. I also find myself feeling some remorse for the victims, and then, on the other hand, I know you will probally think I'm crazy, but I feel some remorse for Volpe himself. I don't know what you know about this case or how much you know. I know through my investigation and through my interrogation that at some point this young man had a deep devoted love for his family and most of all for his mother. I do not know how mentally strong or weak he is. I do know that one man has been convicted of killing five people, and he may not have committed all five murders. I do know that a lot of lives have not only been lost but have been changed for life due to the circumstances. To be honest with you, Tom, in my estimation there's still a lot of questions that need some answering, and I don't know if I have the answers."

"Let me ask you a question, if I can. I may be reaching out far on this, but could this have been a mob hit? From what I know about the North Oak area, I don't think it would be a mob hit from there. What I'm talking about is a mafia hit from Philadelphia. Do you think that is a possibility?"

Lupo found Tom's question strange but curious. He thought to himself maybe he knows something about the Philadelphia syndicate that he doesn't know.

"Well, to be honest with you, Tom, there was some talk about money laundering, loansharking, and unpaid debts that was circling around this investigation. I do have a friend that is working the vice squad down at Sixth and Catherine Street in Philadelphia. I did check with him, and he assured me he knows nothing down there about the murders, only what they read in the papers. I'm sure if there was any type of mafia hit for money that he would've tipped me off about it."

"Tony, did you ever hear of a guy name Carmen Vascello? He goes by the nickname Louie Wash."

"No, I have not."

"Well, I have a cousin who works homicide out of the 39th District in Brooklyn, New York. He called me up several months ago and informed me that there was some action and information going down about the mafia from New York, Philadelphia, and New Jersey. They were bringing in a couple of very dangerous hitman around the time frame of your last two murder victims. The information he gave me was that this gangster named Louis Vascello was brought over from Italy to take care of some loansharking that was going on in one of the suburbs in one of the three major cities in the states. Now, the reason that I mentioned this to you is because this guy Louis. The reason that they call him Louie Wash is because he's very, very clean. He can't be caught. I don't mean to make this more complicated than what it is, Tony. I'm sure you know as well as we all know this mafia thing is a very big organization. Whoever brings these people in from Italy gets them in quick to do their thing, and they get them out a lot faster."

Lupo found Tom's information very interesting. As crazy as it seemed, it made some sense to him He wondered if this could really have happened. Lupo thought maybe not all five murders but just maybe one or two of the victims.

"I do appreciate your concern and your information. Myself, personally, I don't understand how this could happen. I'm not saying that it couldn't have happened, I'm just saying I don't know how. I'll tell you what I want to do though: I will call my friend in Philly and see if he knows anything about this. I want to thank you for taking time with me, and I would just ask one thing again. We keep whatever we said about the murders between the two of us. Please. For now anway. If you hear anything else, here's my card. Please feel free to call me, okay?"

"I will do my best, Tony. It was a pleasure talkin' with you; and if I can help with anything, please don't hesitate to call. Let's keep in touch. I'm looking forward to hearing what you can find out about our murderer.

" Oh, another thing, Tony, remember where you're going, because that's where you'll be." The two men laughed together when Tom said that he knows Tony will need to keep his sense of humor and imagination intact because it's not an easy job that they have. The two men shook hands, said their goodbyes, and Lupo walked out of the office, down the hallway, out of the building, and got into his car, all the time thinking about what Tom had said about Louie Wash.

14 Old Friends Are the Best Friends

The very next day driving to the police station Tony thought that now would be good time to call on his good friend Bob Salvi at the Philadelphia Police Department to find out if he could get more information on the possibility of some organized crime connection in the murders. Lupo knew that it wasn't exactly something that could never have happened. He knew that in some strange way there might be some type of connection to the murders. If not all five murders, possibly something to do with either one or more of the victims themselves or possibly some money laundering that could have gone bad.

Lupo set up a meeting to talk with Bob at one of the diners on the Main Line. Both Tony and Bob knew what the meeting was going to be about, but it also would be good to see each other again. It was about 10:30 on Wednesday morning when Lupo arrived at the Main Line Diner on Bryn Mawr Avenue. It was the type of diner that was right out of the 1930s and 1940s era. The outside of the diner was an old fashion bullet- type train car with shiny silver siding that supported windows all around the diner. The inside had small block-shaped ceramic floor tiles that where dark blue and white. The booths had the oval-shaped tables with light brown vinyl padded benches. The two counter tops were about ten feet long with a countertop made out of formica that stood on either side of the entrance to the double doors that lead into the kitchen area. Around the counter there were round, red vinyl stools that had yellow and white stripes with chrome around the padding and four chrome legs that stood about four feet high. It was the perfect place for two detectives and old friends to meet and talk shop. Tony and Bob were not known in the area, so the men felt very comfortable in what they were about to discuss. When he walked into the diner, Bob Salvi was sitting in the booth at the back of the diner. Bob Salvi was a detective in the Philadelphia Police Department. He worked his way up to a detective who worked on the vice squad and then finally on crime investigations. Bob also was of Italian descent. Both his parents were from Italy. Bob's father was a tailor, originally from Palermo. His father's last name was pronounced Salvitorie but was shortened to Salvi when his parents arrived in America. Bob was a tall handsome man who stood about six feet two inches. He was stocky and had thick black wavy hair. The two men shook hands and laughed as they gave each other a hug, announcing it was good to see one another. When they set down they made some small talk as a waitress came over to take their order. Tony ordered his usual breakfast: black coffee, sausage and scrambled eggs with rye toast. Bob went for black coffee and cream chipped beef. The waitress took down their order and then walked away.

"Bob, it's good to see you. You look good. Is everything's okay? Mary and the kids? Everybody's okay, right?"

"Yeah, Tony, thanks for asking. Everybody's good. We're all in good health, and that's the main thing, right? How about you and your family. Cathy and the kids? Everybody's good? Your mom and dad, are they still doing well?"

"Yeah, we are all good on my end. Thanks for asking and thanks for meeting me. Not only is it good seeing you again, but I got some things I want to talk to you about. I got some ideas I want to run by you to get your feedback. It'll make me understand things possibly a little bit better."

"Sure, Tony, it's always good seeing you again; and whatever I can do to help you, I'm there for you, brother. Now, if I'm correct, you want to talk about the possibility of the evil eye murders that happen in your town being connected to some organized crime, am I right?"

"Yeah, you're right. What's going on, Bob is, with some of the talk around the town and from what our department is hearing, that there may be some kind of mafia connections, to some type of loansharking, money laundering, or whatever. I also am thinking there could be some possible type of drug connection. Now, what I am thinking is that this evil eye curse or belief or whatever the hell you want to call it could really be is some type of cover up to disguise what the real crime may be and that is large amounts of money that was never paid back. Maybe it's money that is due to the mob and maybe this evil eye thing it's just something to throw us off the track of the real issue. It could be loansharking to organized crime people. Now, if that's the case, this "Evil Eye Murder Case" can be bigger than what we originally thought. I wanted to talk to you because I know that you're more involved and have more experience with organized crime than I do. In our department we know that there are some rumblings with organized crime down here in Philly. Before I present anything pertaining to this, I wanted to talk to you first. I wanted to get your feedback on what's going on down there and what your opinion is on my way of thinking with the involvement of organized crime. To be honest with you, Bob, I've been putting a lot of time and energy in on this case. I have been trying to research and look at all different angles. Starting from superstitious beliefs that some people have. I've talked to medical physicians, psychiatrists, whoever I could talk to about superstitious beliefs. Also, as I said before, I'm entertaining the thought of organized crime involvement. So, that's it, my friend. I am here to talk, to listen, and to come away with some type of understanding and hopefully making some type of sense out of this case. Now I will tell you we do have an individual who confessed to the killings. Like I said, with all the talk that we are hearing, I just want to make sure that we have the right person in custody, and that there are no loose ends. Maybe I'm taking it too personally, but it's a case that I want to make sure there's no outside connections, if you know what I'm saying."

"I understand you. Personally, I know about this evil eye thing because some people in my family believe in it and follow some of the tradition. I don't think my mother and father did, and my wife and kids don't. I myself I think it's all bullshit."

"Okay, Bob, we definitely agree on that."

"Now, I will tell you, Tony, there is some action going down in certain sections of the city from organized crime. We know what's going on. We know who the tough guys are and who is a bad ass, and we know who the guys are that think they're tough but are not shit. One guy named Joey Lang thinks he is a tough guy. Yesterday, we picked him up for selling some hot jewelry. He thought he was cute giving us some smart answers, so I smacked him in the back of the head and told him that if he does not wise up he will be doing some real hard time with some real tough ass guys. We started to give him a hard time, and tough guy Joey Lang started to cry like a little baby. That's when I told him he's not a bad ass, he's a punk ass.now, we do know who the people are that are connected, and we do know what they call a captain or lieutenant, and we know who is the head of organized crime down here and what they're into. We know a lot of it is prostitution, loansharking, money laundering, nightclubs, gambling, and possibly drugs."

"Are drugs becoming a big problem down there?"

"From what we're hearing, Tony, is that the drug thing is into the city and could be a big pain in our ass. There also is some talk that there is a possibility in the future that gambling and casinos may come to Atlantic City, so if that happens there could be a lot of bullshit going down with the people in organized crime. We do know one thing: the head of the crime family in South Philly here does not want to deal with or have anything to do with drugs. He is strictly staying in loansharking, gambling, nightclubs, laundering money, and that's it so far. From what we were seeing, you can get your arm or your legs broken if you don't pay back money, or if you're slow paying back the money, or you have a large gambling debt. Now, you know as well as I do if you're not paying back your debt, the mob we'll come down on you and break your bones. If the casinos are coming to Atlantic City, that's going to bring all kinds of hell. We will have people in organized crime fighting for position not only for money, but because they do drugs, and to them the drugs are money. Now what we're seeing if you're on drugs or if you're dealing with large quantity of drugs and something wrong goes down within the crime family, it's real simple Tony: **They're dead.** That's the bottom line. From what we know in the organized crime family, they have what they call soldiers. Apparently soldiers are the ones that either set up or commit the killing. We also know that they've been bringing people in from Sicily, to complete a contract. If two or more families are positioning themselves for territorial rights for the drug trade and to avoid an all out war between the families, they bring negotiators. In certain case the negotiators would dispatch a hostage for a fee to the families that are involved in the negotiations. The hostage involvement was like an insurance policy, and the negotiator was an outside third party involment to try and make sure that both sides of the families were good with the deal. If the deal went south, then both the negotiator and the hostage would be killed. Then the family who sent the negotiator and the hostage would take revenge on the people who were responsible for killing both the negotiator and the hostage. Now that, my friend, is no evil eye superstition, and you can believe that. I have to be honest with you, Tony. I myself have not heard on the street anything about this evil eye curse or about any type of superstition."

" I didn't think you would. I think something about that type of superstition could some way only be related to the "Evil Eye Murder Case" in North Oak, at least for now. Let me ask you a question. Did you ever hear of how organized crime sets up a hit for hire and how the hell do they get away with it?"

"No, I don't know. All we know is that they bring people in from Sicily. They set them up in whatever city or town where the contract is supposed to be completed. We don't know how long they're here. It could be for a day, a week, months, whatever to study or observe the person or people they have the contract on. We believe that after they have enough information on the person or persons that the contract is out on, then they will kill them and leave the country that very same day. They're in and out, quick and fast. These people are professionals. We can tell a professional hit from someone that don't know what the hell they're doing and just wants to murder somebody because they're pissed off. This is serious business, Tony. This is loansharking, gambling, or someone trying to move in on someone's territory, or to move up in the ranks of organized crime. That's what I know and what we know downtown. Now, if you're asking me if I believe that someone would murder some people because of an evil eye curse, I'd have to say—being a cop for as long as I have and knowing what I know—it would not surprise me at all."

"I know, Bob, I agree with you. Nothing surprises me today, nothing at all."

"Tony, from what you've been telling me and the little bit that I know, the only thing that I can say about that case is that the individual you have if he confessed to the murders, it's one thing. My concern would be why did it take five or six years to catch him. Could he be taking the rap for someone else? Possibly. You have a lot of questions, and maybe you'll find **some** of the answers, but I do not think you will find **all** of the answers. I will tell you this, my friend, things like this happen in life, and we will never be able to figure it out. The only thing we can do is just try to correct the wrong the best we can, so guys like you and I can sleep at night."

"Yeah, I agree with, you, Bob. From talking with other people involved in law enforcement, it's mostly the same thing that I am hearing. The thing that I have to get control of is that I'm hearing a lot of different aspects of the murder. I'm hearing about people coming in to town from Italy to take care of some debt. I was talking to a detective in Upper Merion Township about a murder investigation of a 12-year-old girl, and the detective started up about the evil eye murders. He mentioned an man's name; he called him Louie Wash. He said almost exactly what you said about bringing these people in from Sicily to complete a contract. So now, what I have to do is try to digest this and come up with my own conclusions. I don't know what it is or why it is, but for some reason this evil eye case has my attention more so than any other case that I worked before. I sometimes think that it's because of my Italian heritage and that it happened so close to home that I sometimes get emotionally involved in the case."

"Tony, listen to me for a minute. We've been friends for a long time. Remember the high school days playing football, our cars, our girlfriends, the guys we hung around with? It was always me and you that wanted to be in law enforcement. Because we wanted to try and make a difference. We wanted to help people. We wanted to help the person who could not help himself. We came from good families. We had great family values. We had a good Catholic upbringing. We do our best, you and I. We worked our way up from patrolmen to detectives. We're both lieutenants. We make a good salary and good living. We have to use our judgment. We have to use our knowledge and our God-given talent. We can only work with what we are given to work with. You and I both know there's all kinds rumors when a crime goes down, especially a murder. With this murder in a small town like North Oak—that really isn't that small—all kind a hell breaks loose. You're going to hear all kinds of rumors. People are going to be saying this and saying that, and most of it is going to be bullshit. You know I'm not telling you something you don't already know, but I will tell you this: To get emotionally involved in a case such as the "Evil Eye Murder Case," to get emotionally involved with the victims or the murderer himself is something I personally try not to do. My friend, I feel you should not let it happen to you."

"I get what you're saying, and I tried to follow along those lines. I just want to make sure that for the murderer and the victims I did the best I could. I know everything you're saying is true, Bob. We are good people, and we have no crystal ball to go by. I'm glad we met and I talked to you because it's always good talking to a good friend and someone who understands what we do, how we do it, and why we do it."

"We do it, Tony, because we both like what we do. Now, when the time comes when either you or I don't like what we do, that we're tired of all the hatred, the murders, the beatings, the abuse, and all the bullshit that goes on in any town or city, when we are truly tired of it, Tony, that's when we get the hell out. That's when we can say we did our best. That's all we can do. We say, 'I've had enough, it's time for me to retire.' So, we close that chapter on that part of our lives and then we start a new life away from all this miserable and nasty bullshit. Right now, we deal with some of the scum that you and I deal with, but this is not no bank job, Tony. This is not an 8:00 to 5:00 office job. It's not a "Donna Reed" or "My Three Sons" TV show of a big wide beautiful town or city in America where the only problem for the local police department of the town or city is that somebody's kitty cat is caught up a tree or somebody's little son Junior got caught playing hooky from school that day. It's no wonderland, Tony, you know it and I know it. There are not too many guys we knew growing up who could deal with the bullshit, with the crime and with the misery that's out on some of the streets where we live, and that's a fact. I know for me the only thing that gets me by is my family, and I know that some day I may help a little kid riding a bicycle or an old lady who just got robbed out of her Social Security check. I can help her get her money back, and we put that prick who robbed her away, and that is what makes me feel good."

"I know you're right, and the funny thing is I agree with everything you're saying. There are times that I think about getting out and I think about retiring, but it's like you said, if I can help some poor helpless person out there that some prick is going to rob, beat up, molest, or kill, well that's when my dago temper gets the best of me, and I want to see the son of a bitch looking at me from the other side of the bars when his ass is in a jail cell, and I'm standing there and I say to him, 'How do you like the view from your new home?' So you're right, Bob we both want to help the best we can."

" I'm glad you talk with me because, as always, it's good to see you, man. You know something, Tony, we really did good for ourselves with our families and with our wives. Mary and Cathy were good girls in high school and are good ladies now and are very good mothers. Think about this. Some guys we know want to marry the prom queen and some guys end up with a witch. I'll talk to Mary. Maybe we'll get together in a couple weeks with you and Cathy and we'll go out for dinner. I've been wanting to try this Italian place called Ralph's, supposed to be the best veal in the city."

"That sounds good to me. I'll tell Cathy to give Mary a call, and we will set it up in a couple weeks for a Saturday night. Listen, Bob, thanks again for all your help and support. I will keep you informed, and let you know how I make out. Please tell Mary and the kids I said hello."

15 Uncle Carlo

As he was driving back to North Oak from the Main Line after talking with his friend Bob, Lupo had a thought. Maybe it was time for him to call his Uncle Carlo Vanbessai in Brooklyn. Lupo knew his uncle was invovled in union and construction business and possibly some activities connected with racketeering. He knew that, if there would be any connection with the underworld, maybe his Uncle Carlo would know if some type of activity could be connected with the evil eye murders or with this hitman Louie Wash. He also knew and tried to understand that he didn't and couldn't get emotionally involved. It was just something that he needed to be sure of. He also understood that, if the murders we're connected in some way to the mafia, it would open up a whole new can of worms. It very well could be something that a small town like North Oak may not be able to handle.

The very next day at 8:35 AM when Detective Lupo arrived in his office at the North Oak Police Department, he walked over to the coffee pot and got himself a cup of black coffee, went over to his desk, and looked at his Rolodex for his Uncle Carlo's phone number. When he found the number, he pulled the card from the Rolodex, placed it down next to his phone, then began to call his uncle. The phone rang three times when a voice on the other end said, "Hello."

"Hello, Aunt Mary, it's Anthony Lupo. How are you doing this morning? I hope I didn't wake you up."

" Hello, Anthony, good to hear from you... no no no you didn't wake me. I've been up since 6 o'clock. I'm eating breakfast with Uncle Carlo. How are you doing? Is everything all right with your family, your mom and dad?"

"Oh, yeah, we are doing good Aunt Mary. Mom and Dad are still healthy, thank God. Cathy and our kids are doing well, and they are getting big. They're eating us out of house and home."

Tony and the rest of the Lupo family would see his Uncle Carlo and Aunt Mary's family only periodically through the years. Although they were not related by blood, they still respected each other's families and would address them as Aunt Mary and Uncle Carlo. Uncle Carlo was a large sized, brawny man with olive skin, thick salt and pepper hair, who sported a thick black mustache. He spoke with a little Italian accent and enjoyed smoking handmade cigar from his favorite cigar shop called Havana Nick's on Seventh and State Street in Brooklyn. Aunt Mary was a slender, very attractive lady for her age. She had thick jet black hair and also had olive skin. She spoke very softly and always had a smile whenever she talked with someone. She was born in Sicily. She called into the kitchen and said to Carlo, "It's your nephew, Anthony Lupo, who would like to talk to you." It was at that time when Carlo walked from the kitchen into the living room with his coffee cup in one hand and grabbed the phone from Mary with the other.

"Hello, Anthony, how are you today? It's good to hear from you. Is everything all right?"

"Hello, Uncle Carlo, everything is fine. I hope I am not disturbing your breakfast. I was just wondering if I could talk to you about a case I'm working on that I feel you might have some imput for me?"

"Sure, Anthony, that will be fine. As a matter of fact, Aunt Mary and I will be down your way this evening. Aunt Mary's sister Marie is in the hospital. You know, having some women problems, so we're going down to visit her and are going to stay a few days so Mary can help her out. Going to be down in the town of Wayne. Actually, it's funny, I was going to call your father when I got down there. I was hoping to get together with him. If you like, we can meet somewhere. I don't know how far Wayne is from where you live?"

"That will be great, Uncle Carlo. Wayne is not far from where I live at all. Actually there's a diner on Lancaster Avenue in Wayne where we can meet and discuss what I'd like to talk to you about. Would Sunday be okay for you, say around 11 o'clock or so?"

"Sure, Anthony, that'll work for me. Will your father be with you?"

"No, Uncle Carlo, if it's okay with you. I'd just like to talk to you one on one. Is that all right?"

"Oh, yeah, that will be good for sure. I'll call your father and I'll meet him some other time. I'm sure he will understand."

"Great. Thank you, and I'll see you on Sunday. Have a safe drive down and give my love and regards to Aunt Mary and your family. Goodbye."

At 11 o'clock on Sunday morning Detective Lupo arrived at Maggio's Diner. Lupo was sitting in the booth with a side window so he could look out and see the cars that pulled into the parking lot. He ordered one of his favorites: a piece of apple pie with a cup of black coffee. At about 11:15 he saw his Uncle Carlo pulling up in the parking lot and noticed he was driving a brand-new 1967 black Cadillac Coup-De-Ville. As he pulled the car up to parking spot and got out, he could see his nephew looking out at him shaking his head and laughing. His uncle waved to him and started to laugh as he walked up the steps to enter the diner.. Lupo stood up to greet his uncle with a smile, shook his hand as the two men hugged each other, and then Lupo kissed him on the cheek. They made some small talking about the families and laughed together as Carlo ordered a cup of black coffee with rye toast.

"Listen, Uncle Carlo, it's always good to see you. Thank you for coming and meeting me like this."

"Hey, no a problem, Anthony. It's always good to see you. Is everything all right? I hope there's no problem."

" Oh, yeah, yeah everything is good, Uncle Carlo. I wanted to talk to you one-on-one because I've been working on a murder case for about six years now and we have a individual in jail. The murder case happened in my hometown, and the newspapers in town are calling it "The Evil Eye Murder Case." As I said, we have someone who is incarcerated now, but I'm hearing and seeing that there's a lot of loopholes. There's been some talk around town that this person was not the only killer and that there may have been others. Also, there's been some talk about some connections possibly to the underworld and the possibility of some loansharking. Now, I come to you, Uncle Carlo— I hope you don't mind—because I know what you do, and I know you'll be straight up with me because there's word out on the street and from other law enforcement sections about a man who takes care of business with money laundering, loansharking, and unpaid debts, if you know what I mean. I'm at my wits end, and I truly feel bad about talking to you about this. I don't want to offend you, but I am hoping you can shine some light on the information I have."

"Anthony, listen to me, you do not offend me. I told your father if he ever needs me for anything I would be there for him and his family, so that goes for you too. Your father knows what I do and obviously you do too. Anthony you must believe me and understand that I have the highest respect for your father and his family and for you being in lawn enforcement. I don't make any excuses, Anthony for what I do, and you know your father and I came to this country from Italy. It's true we both did some things with money to help each other out. Back in the day people were bringing a lot of family members over from the old country and helping them out financially. Some people were fortunate and were able to pay the money back. Other people wanted interest on their money. It's a shame because it made things for families hard to make ends meet. Now, Anthony, your father and I helped a lot of people, but we did nothing to hurt people only to help them get into America. Yes, it's true there were people that helped both your father and I out financially. But I assure you, Anthony, your father and I and some of my other acquaintances did not do anything that was controlled by the underworld. Your father raised three children the right way, the proper way in America. My wife and I, we raised three children the right and proper way in this country. This is a great country: the land of the free and the home of the brave. My son Michael graduated from Cornell University and works now as an accountant for one of the bigger law firms in the city. My daughter Angela is a graduate from college also. She is a pharmacist and a manager of a drug company in Chicago. Now, my son Salvatore, also a college boy, runs our family business now that I'm retired. He takes care of our construction company located in Manhattan. We are doing very well, thank God. So you see, Anthony, we were all blessed when we came to America. Your father and mother were blessed with children. We all had an opportunity to do good for ourselves. I am sorry I don't mean to keep talking. So what is the information that you have that you feel I can help you with?"

"I've been hearing about a man who has been taking care of business dealing with the rackets, loansharking, and possibly some money laundering. My concern is if this person is involved some way with the evil eye murders because the murders somehow are connected with unpaid debts and money that was not ever paid back. I'm also hearing about bringing people over from Sicily to take care of some of the money problems that some of these people have. I don't know if there's people or one person involved, but the one person whose name I do know—and it has come up in law enforcement—is a man name Louis Wash."

"Anthony, I'm going to tell you something and it's true. I don't know if your father ever told you how we met and became friends."

"To tell you the truth, Uncle Carlo, my father never told me anything about that. All we knew was that you're my brother's Godfather and we always called you Uncle Carlo and Aunt Mary."

" I am Godfather to your older brother Salvatore, and your father and mother are Godparents to my daughter Angela. Your father and I met on a ship that was leaving Sicily and heading for America. Your father had gotten in a little trouble with another fellow on the ship. I interfered and helped him out, and we became friends. Your father and I are both from Sicily. What I'm about to tell you now, Anthony, should stay between me and you. Ok?"

"Sure. Whatever is said here today is strictly between you and me. You have my word on that."

"Good, Anthony, very good. My family and I owned a restaurant/nightclub in Italy. There was great food and good music all the time. Let me tell you, the place was doing well. I was part owners with my cousins, Angelo and Carmen. One day I received a call from my cousin Angelo who told me that one of the two fellas who were running the nightclub was skimming money off the top. He told me that he and Carmen wanted to see me at 11:30 Sunday morning in the nightclub. So Sunday morning came around, I got in my car, and I went to meet my two cousins at the nightclub. When I got there, my cousin's car was there, and I noticed some other vehicle parked in the parking lot. I parked my car, walked into the restaurant, and down the steps to the nightclub. When I walked into the nightclub, my two cousins were sitting at a table with one of the fellas, Sabino who was running the nightclub. I walked over to the table and sat down. My cousin Carmen said to Sabino. 'Where is Raphael?' Sabino said to him, 'He's in the back checking the list for the booze order.' Carmen told him, 'I want you to go back and get him, I want to talk to him.' When Sabino went back to get Raphael, I had a very strange feeling. I asked my two cousins what was going on. My cousin Carmen looked over at me and said to me, 'I'll take care of this' When Sabino and Raphael came out of the back and sat down at the table with myself and my two cousins, Raphael looked at my cousin Carmen and said, 'What's up.' At that very moment my cousin Carmen pulled out a gun and **BOOM** he shot Raphael once in the head. As Raphael fell off the chair onto the floor, he turned the gun and pointed it in Sabino's face and said, 'Now, if you try and take any money from us you bastard, I will kill you too. Now, get the hell out of here.' Sabino got up, and he left. My cousin Carmen took a quick shot of whiskey, looked at me and my cousin Angelo, and said, 'I'll see you tomorrow. I have some other business to take care of, ok and he walked out of the club. My cousin Angelo and I just looked at each other. We both were stunned. That's when my cousin Angelo said to me, 'Louis is one crazy son of a bitch.' I tell you something now, Anthony. My cousin Carmen's full name is Carmen Louis Vascello. He is called and he is known as

LOUIE WASH. After Carmen killed Raphael, I knew it was time for myself and my family to leave all that bullshit behind."

"Uncle Carlo, do you know whatever happened to Carmen after he killed Raphael. Did he ever do time for the murder?"

"I don't know, Anthony, and I don't care. I just wanted to get the hell out of that place as fast as I could. So that's when I took my wife and two children and we left for America. I don't know anymore today about my cousin Angelo or Carmen. Some years ago I did have brief contact with my cousin Angelo, and he informed me that Carmen had been doing some work for certain people in Italy and America also. As you said, with this 'Evil Eye Murder Case' the killings were from the early 1960s to the mid 1960s. I do know this, that Carmen was in America around that time and that's all I know."

"Uncle Carlo, I really need to know is there's anything else around that time that you can tell me. Was Carmen in Pennsylvania anywhere near Philadelphia?"

"Anthony, listen to me. Carmen is a crazy son of a bitch. I want you to have no illusions, none at all, as to what type of person he is. For all I know, he could be dead by now. People that deal in that type of business are either in one or two places: JAIL OR DEAD."

"Okay, Uncle Carlo, I thank you for your time and whatever was said between us will stay with us. I know deep down in my heart that my father is a good man, and I know he would not do anything to harm someone. I also know that you are good man. It's just that this evil eye case is a case that I want to make sure I connect all the dots. It had our whole town in a big uproar. Some people were scared to death. They were afraid to go out their front doors, and I want to try my best to get closure with all the buzz that is going around."

"Anthony, listen to me, this evil eye bullshit is mostly followed by people who are weak of heart, people who are scared, people with very little faith. There were Italian people and families in New York and in the old country who would believe in this evil eye curse. Probably people not just in Italy, but I'm sure around the world who killed people because of a curse. It's crazy. Me personally, I think it's all a bunch of bullshit. People should believe in God and not this evil eye crap. There is an old Italian saying that goes like this: **Remember one thing when you point your finger at someone, there's three fingers pointing back at you.** Some people want to point their finger, some people want to talk about people and make up lies, and some people are never happy, they're just some miserable sons of bitches. I'm sure you're doing the best you can. You're not only a damn good police officer, you're a very very good human being. My advice to you is do the best you can, but don't go crazy and beat yourself up about it. Because in life if you do the best you can and in your heart you believe you did the best you can, then that's all that matters. I have to go now, Aunt Mary is making some homemade *pasta e faggiola* tonight for dinner, and I told her I would only be out a couple of hours. Oh, by the way, I did call your father and I'm going to meet him Tuesday. Aunt Mary and I are going to take him and your mother out for dinner."

"Once again, Uncle Carlo, thank you for your time and the information. Please give Aunt Mary my love and regards and tell your family I said hello. Oh, and by the way, I know about that old Italian saying my father said it to me a long time ago, and I always try to remember not to point my finger at anyone."

The two men got up from the booth, shook hands, and hugged each other. As they were walking out of the diner, they made some small talk as they walked to their cars.

16 Monsignor Avandonto

Things were not going well at home between Cathy and Tony. In Cathy's mind it seemed like Tony was just not himself. There was a great deal of tension between them. Cathy was concerned about him; she felt that he was spending too much time on the "Evil Eye Murder Case." She was having a hard time understanding why he was dedicating so much time at work and on the case when she knew they had already had the person who committed the murders in jail. He was waking up at night which was very unusual for him. When Cathy would ask him why he was waking up, was he sick, did he feel all right, Tony's only answer to his wife was, "Go back to sleep. I'm okay. Don't worry." He wasn't eating properly and when Cathy would asked him if everything was okay, he just told her he was not that hungry and for her not to worry. Tony wasn't spending time with the family or playing with the children. He had actually forgotten some of the school functions that his children were involved with. When Cathy would bring it up to him, he would say, "I'm very busy at work. I'm okay. Don't worry." Cathy, being a loving wife, a supportive wife, a good mother, knew that Tony was spreading things too thin. She took it upon herself to call Monsignor Avandonto and asked him if he could talk to Tony as a favor for her. The monsignor was more than glad to talk to him. He was very close to both of them and the Lupo family in general. Cathy had told Tony that Monsignor Avandonto called and asked for him and that he wanted to talk about something. As usual, Tony was under the impression that he was going to talk to the monsignor about another function that the church was going to sponsor. The time seemed to be right for Tony to talk with Monsignor Avandonto who was the pastor of Saint Francis Catholic Church in North Oak. Tony knew the monsignor well from the charitable organizations that the church would hold for the less fortunate people in the parish and the surrounding town. Most of the catholic churches in North Oak would sponsor various types of functions for the local parishioners to attend. Some of the functions that were held by the various catholic churches in North Oak were a way for them to raise money to support the churches and also to help the less fortunate parishioners. Tony and some of the police officer friends who belonged to Saint Francis were very active in their parish charitable functions. As usual, Tony Lupo dedicated a lot of time to charitable organizations that the church sponsored. Some of the organizations were at various times of the year.

All of the church functions were held inside the auditorium which was connected to the church. In October the church would have a Halloween party. In November the church sponsored what they called their turkey day dinner. December had the largest attendance for the December Christmas celebration. Then the Easter parade breakfast. All the children would have an Easter egg hunt and receive an Easter basket. The final event was in July: The church carnival was held on the second weekend of July. This function was a way for the catholic church to receive revenue from this three-day affair to support the catholic church financial status.

The monsignor had set up a meeting for Wednesday morning at 10:30 in his office at the rectory. Tony arrived at the rectory about five after 10. He walked up to the front porch, rang the doorbell, and Mary DePalma opened the door and greeted Tony as she told him to enter. Mary was an elderly, heavyset Italian lady with white hair that fell just below her ears. She wore wire rimmed glasses, and she always wore an apron that hung around her neck and was tied around her waist. No matter who went over to the rectory to speak to Monsignor or any of the other priests who lived there, you could always count on Mary DePalma to greet them with a smile and a very crisp hello. Tony and Mary exchanged greetings and some laughter as Tony walked into the hallway of the rectory. She informed Tony that the monsignor was upstairs and he'd be right down as she escorted him into the study. The rectory at Saint Francis, built in the 1940's, was constructed of beautiful stone. Attached to the rectory was a large front porch with a large oak front door and a stained glass window on either side of the door.

As Tony was sitting in this study waiting for the monsignor to come in, he noticed how beautiful and quiet it was inside the rectory. The only sound that he could hear was the sound of Mary and another lady talking about what they were going to make for dinner to serve the clergy that evening. The other sound Tony noticed was the sound of the good monsignor walking down to his study to greet him.

"Good morning, Monsignor, it's good to see you. How are you feeling today?"

"Good morning, Tony. I'm doing very well today; and as usual, it is always good to see you, my friend. How is the family doing? Cathy and the kids and your job, everything is okay?"

"Yes, Monsignor, Cathy and the kids are doing well: healthy and happy. The job is ok. If it is not one thing, it is another. That's how it is with police work."

The two men talked and made friendly conversation for a few minutes. The conversations went from politics, talking about who got elected as the mayor of North Oak, to sports and how the Philadelphia Eagles were doing, the Philadelphia Phillies, and so on. They talked about the town, about new buildings being constructed. They talked about how the King of Prussia area was starting to grow and become a metropolis. Then Monsignor Avandonto mentioned to Tony about his police work, and he asked if he knew why he had wanted to see him. Tony responded to the monsignor that he was under the imperssion it may have been for a function that he would need support with. With that in mind, the monsignor looked at Tony and said that he wanted to talk to him about his police work.

"Let's start out first and foremost for you and I to be on a first name basis. So please call me by my first name so we both can become comfortable with one another. I appreciate your respect, but for now you can forget the monsignor part; it will just be Tony and Vince if that's okay with you?"

"Sure, I'm fine with that. I will call you Vince."

"Good. The reason I asked you to meet with me was because your wife Cathy talked to me the other day, and she seemed a bit concerned. She seems to be concerned about your health and your well-being. I want you to know that whatever we talk about will stay between us. You're not at confession. This is just two guys talking, listening, hoping to help one another."

As the monsignor was talking, all Tony could think about was if there really is a family problem. Was the problem with Cathy and him, him and the kids, or was it work related? He also was wondering why his wife got involved. He always knew that whatever it was with the family, whether it was Cathy and him or with the kids, they could always work things out. How bad could it be that she had to come to speak to Monsignor Avandonto?

"Tony, Cathy was talking to me about your involvement in a murder case that happened several years ago. I believe the case was called "The Evil Eye Murder Case." I can tell you this: When I came to this parish and I took over for the pastor at that time, he enlightened me about the impact that this murder case had on our parish and our community. I'm sure you're aware that when something like this happens it can be extremely difficult for people to get over. It's also very difficult for people to try and understand why. Cathy is concerned that your involvement with the case has continued long after the case has closed. Apparently, from what I understand, they caught the person invovled in the murders. He pleaded guilty to the murders; and according to Cathy and some of people in our community, it is an open and shut case. With all due respect, the case is closed. Now, my question to you Tony is am I to understand that the case is closed, or in your opinion or in our police department's opinion it's not an open and shut case as the people believe it is."

"Well, let me start out by saying, I thank you for taking time out of your busy schedule to talk to my wife, and I want apologize if it cost any undue aggravation to you because I know being the monsignor of a parish this size you have a lot of issues that have to be addressed, so I thank you again."

"Thank you for your concern, and let me be clear, this is no inconvenience for me to first speak to Cathy or to speak with you. You and Cathy have a great family. You and the North Oak Police Department have been very good to our parish and very good to the underprivileged people in our parish, so please don't apologize either for yourself , for the Police Department, or for Cathy. Now, please continue. I'd like to try and understand whole heartedly so I can help in anyway."

"It's true that I am having some difficulty trying to close this case completely. It's also true that we do have a person in prison who has pleaded guilty to the murders. However, through my investigations—and I've been on this case for several years—there is still some question that maybe the person convicted of the murders did not act alone. Let me elaborate a little more on that statement. There were questions that he may have had help with the murders simply because in all five of the murders there were no signs of breaking in."

"Well, Tony, I do understand your concern and possibly your theory and the department's theory on the breaking and entering. If my memory serves me right, I myself spoke to Father DeVille somewhat about this murder, as I said before, and as I recollect, I believe that you also spoke to Father DeVille to some extent about the case. Would I be correct on this? Was he any help, and did he answer all of your concerns?"

"Yes, you are correct, and he was a great deal of help. Actually, what father De Ville and I spoke about was what is the relationship between faith and fear. As I recollect, both of us wondered if the killings were committed out of fear. I fully understand what Father DeVille was saying; but my concern is not necessarily the motive of fear but was there actually only the one perpetrator and was fear the only reason. I have this crazy notion, Vince that fear could have been the foundation of the murders, but there could also have been a good deal of financial interest involved in the case. By that, I mean money laundering, loansharking, and money that was not paid back. Also, for some crazy reason I believe it could have been done out of love."

"Out of love? I don't understand what you mean by out of love. Are you talking about the type of love between a man and a woman?"

"Well, to be honest with you, and I'm not trying to complicate this case any further, I believe it could have been fear or money. I also believe it may have been about love. By that I mean the love that a son has for his mother and his family. See, when Father DeVille and I had our conversation at that time, we didn't even know or have a suspect. The good father was talking about the evil eye superstition, and we were talking about faith and fear. If I'm not mistaken, the killings he suggested could have been committed out of fear. Now, if I may explain further on my theory, I'd like to continue."

"Please, Tony, continue. It sounds interesting, and I want to hear what you have to say from your perspective."

"Thank you. As I was saying, from some of the information that I received on this case and the way I understand it, the murderer's family was harassed either with fear about the evil eye curse or fear about money issues that we're not paid or both. In any case, most of it was noted that they were harassed around the holiday. In our investigation all of the five victims were killed around the holidays. There was also speculation that the suspect's mother was going through the change of life. We do not know whether that played a part in what this young man was thinking about. I really don't know. We tried to follow-up as many leads as we could. All I'm saying is that I know Italian families, I know my family, and holidays are special to us, to our parents, our children. It is special to all of us. I do know and I am trying to understand fear and money problems. I do understand that these type of issues or problems can make a person get at the end of their rope. I guess that's why Cathy would like me to talk to you because I'm getting involved in a second and possibly even a third person suspect theory. We at the department and I myself have been receiving information about some underworld involvement and that's why the money issue has come up. All five of these killings were of old people that were in business for themselves and well off financially. Now, all the killings where cold-blooded calculated murders. They were over a period of years. Everyone of them was shot in the head at least once or twice, and it was very strategically planned out."

"Tony, I believe you have a very valid point. Although I must tell you that you have to have faith. I believe strongly that fear simply comes from not having faith. Either faith in yourself, faith in others, and most strongly faith in God. From what I know of this, I agree with Father DeVille about faith and fear. I only know from the information that I received from Father DeVille and in the newspapers. I will agree with Father DeVille that people could commit crimes out of fear, and I will also agree with you that people can commit crimes out of love. Tony, I'm sure you know that there have been crimes of passion. There have been wars over love, there have been many battles, and many unseen circumstances committed either because of love or over love. Yes, perhaps this young man committed this crime because of love for his mother, for the devotion he had for his family.

"As far as the money aspect you're speaking of all I can say to you is the one word... **GREED**. I try not to involve myself with disrespectful and unscrupulous people from our Italian heritage, those involved in such underworld practices. I would be naïve, Tony, to tell you that I do not believe this type of greed happens today. You, my friend, are the detective, you are the investigator, I'm sure it's a great deal on you to figure out who committed this crime. You are the one that has to figure out if it is a crime of passion, if it is a crime of fear, or if it is a crime of greed. You are the one that has this task to figure out who committed what murder or how many murders and for what reason. That is a hard decision for you to make; but with your faith, I am sure you will make the right decision. Now, if you stop and think about this for a moment, you're back to what you and Father De Ville spoke about when you and he were discussing faith and fear. Actually, Tony, your faith in Cathy and her faith in you as a good husband could have been what brought you to speak with me. So, we must believe that your faith will make you feel at ease about the questions you have about this murder case. I also believe that with the faith that you and Cathy have for each other, it will all work out.

"Now, about the murders and all the people involved, I am sorry to say I really don't have the answer as to why and when things of this nature happen. I'm sure that Father DeVille tried the best he could to explain the catholic faith and our catholic ways of understanding life and the belief that some people have about fear. I, myself, as a religious person, I try and teach and I try to preach when I'm on the pulpit the ways of the Ten Commandments. You know, Tony, in life from the very beginning of the world to the very end, people will agree and disagree. People will understand and people will not understand; but I must say, if you follow the Ten Commandments that God has given us, no matter what religion, no matter what belief, with the Ten Commandments you cannot go wrong. In our society we have kings, presidents, emperors, queens and so on. People who will make rules, regulations, and laws about what we as human beings must do. If we do not follow the rules, regulations, and laws, then we will have complete anarchy. What I preach and what I as a servant of the Lord abide by are the Ten Commandments. My faith lies within the Ten Commandments. So what I say to you now, my friend, is you follow God's Ten Commandments you will be fine."

"I understand, Vince, fully what you're saying. The situation that I am questioning is not only the fear of this evil eye superstition, I'm questioning the involvement with money and the second or possibly third person suspect involvement. That's the problem that I'm struggling with. I want to truly believe and hope we arrested the right person who committed the murders. But the question that nags at me. Is he the only person who committed the murders and that's where I'm at now. To be quite honest, Vince, that's the reason that Cathy, my wonderful wife, the mother of my beautiful children, my family that I need so very much, is concerned about my mental and physical health and why she respectfully requested that you speak to me. Thank you very much for taking the time to talk to me. I know that I can only do my best, and I'll be happy with that because my best is all I can give. I do understand that no matter how hard I try, life will go on and I will be satisfied and happy that I know I gave it my best."

"Tony, let me leave you with one thing: You are a good man and you have a wonderful family. Your children are good in school, and you bring them up in the catholic tradition. Your wife is concerned and that's why she spoke to me. I am glad we had this conversation. I understand from your perspective and I believe you understand from mine. Without sounding redundant, the only thing I could tell you my friend is that the Ten Commandments are the laws that we were given. Believe me, if we follow the laws of the Ten Commandments, I believe that we as a society will not go wrong. You are very fortunate that your catholic faith has kept you strong. It's not fear, because fear simply does not keep you strong. Fear is a weakness inside, and I believe in my heart that people can go through life either having fear about one thing or another. Having faith is what helps us combat fear. Your parents raised you to be a good individual and you're doing the same with your family. The only thing I can leave you with now is go out with the grace of God and be safe; your answers will come. God bless you. Faith will conquer all. I would like to end this meeting with a prayer."

"Thank you, Vince, I would like that."

17 Sergeant Baker

t was 8:30 AM on a Tuesday morning: a cold, damp, and dreary day. There was still a fog hovering over the surrounding Philadelphia area. It was the kind of day that was gray, cloudy, the kind of weather that would chill you to your bones. As Lupo was walking into the office, his partner in crime, Chubbs, announced to him that he had just got off the phone with Sergeant Baker who wanted to talk to him. Lupo asked Chubbs if he told him what it was about. All he told him was that he wanted Lupo to give him a call as soon as he could. Lupo nodded that he understood what he said as he was taking off his trench coat and was walking over to the coat rack to hang it up. He started thinking to himself, *Who the hell is Sergeant Baker?* Lupo knew almost all of the sergeants, lieutenants, and captains on the police force. After he hung up his coat and laid his hat on top of the coat rack, he walked over and picked up the message that Chubbs had handed him with Sergeant Baker's phone number on it. Lupo then walked over to the coffee area and got himself a cup of coffee. He grabbed himself a piece of coffee cake and walked back to his desk. The whole time he was still wondering who Sergeant Baker is. Lupo asked Chubbs if he knew who this Sergeant Baker was. Chubbs replied, "He's the tall black cop, Don Baker, who just made sergeant several weeks ago." Lupo realized who Sergeant Baker was as he was taking a bite of his coffee cake and taking a sip of his coffee. He sat down at his desk, pulled out the piece of paper from his shirt pocket, and dialed the phone number to talk to Sergeant Baker. Eating his coffee cake and drinking his cup of coffee, the phone rang. It was on the third ring that Sergeant Baker picked up.

"Hello, Vice Squad. Sergeant Baker speaking. How can I help you?"

"Sergeant Baker, this is Detective Lupo. I got your message and am returning your call. First of all, I'd like to congratulate you on making sergeant and to wish you good luck."

"Thank you, Detective, that was one of the reasons that I called you. To thank you for anything you did for me or any pull you had to help me along the road here. I made sergeant and got my new assignment in vice squad here about a month ago. So, I apologize for not calling you right away. Thank you again for any help and support you may have given."

"All I really did, Sergeant, was tell the chief how you had my back that night behind the station, and I thought you were a good and upright officer. It really comes down to you yourself passing the test. You did a good job, and I'm glad you made sergeant. I personally believe it couldn't happen to a nicer fella, and I'm glad you're on the force with us Sergeant Baker. I believe you're going to do well."

"Well, thank you, Detective, and please call me Don. There was another reason for my calling. I remember our conversation that we had that evening; and if you remember, I brought up to you that over on my side of town the black folks know about the evil eye murders and about capturing the person and the possibility that there could be some other people involved in the murders. Do you remember talking about that with me?"

"Yes, I do remember, Don. You and I just briefly talked about it, and please call me, Tony. So what is on your mind about the murders?"

Don Baker had Lupo's undivided attention. Lupo was always ready, willing, and able to talk to anyone who may have some insight on either the murderers victims, the murderer, or other suspects. He was very sure to pay close attention to what Don Baker was going to tell him."

"It was a few weeks ago and I was tagging along with a detective by the name of Al Taylor; he's from the vice squad, and he says he knows you."

"Yeah, I know Al well. He is a good man. If you're working with him, you'll learn a lot. I think he's been on vice for a while, if I'm not mistaken." Lupo wanted him to get back to his take on the murders. "We were up in Reading, Al and I, shadowing some detectives when a call came in about 1:00 or 1:30 in the morning. There was some commotion down at this very up-scale brothel on the north end of town. When we got there, there were two police detectives from the Reading barracks and two other police officers in a patrol car for backup. Al and I entered the place and were talking to some of the girls. Apparently, there was some commotion with one or two guys who did not want to pay for their pleasures, if you know what I mean. As two of the detectives from Reading were questioning one girl, I happened to recognize one of the girls that was working at this place. She's was a local girl who was from North Oak, so I started talking to her. At first we started talking about what happened with the two guys and why they wouldn't pay. As I got more involved in the conversation with her, she brought up something about a customer she had dealt with several months ago. At the time I didn't think much about what she was saying until she mentioned that her client was from Italy, and he was only here for a short time. She also mentioned that he used the words 'evil eye'. Now, I don't know if it's anything important or if I'm just grabbing at straws, but I just thought maybe you might be interested in talking with her. I just thought she might have some information that you can use."

"You said that this girl you were talking to came from over your part of town. How well do you know her and can she be trusted?"

"I basically knew her from my neighborhood. I knew her growing up. We went to the same grade school and high school together. To be honest with you, Tony, and this is strictly between you and me. We became friendly, if you know what I mean. She grew up in an unusual situation, I might add. The story was that her father was a black guy who was a star football player and a very good athlete at North Oak High School back in the day. Her mother was a white girl who was a cheerleader for the football team back then. He got the girl pregnant, and she had to leave school to have the baby. The kid had a pretty rough life. Her mother came from an Italian family. From what I understand, her family did not want to know anything about the baby. She and her mother were on their own with no help from the family or anybody else for that matter. Unfortunately for the girl, her mother passed away. We never heard anymore about where the father was. Some of the kids were tough on her in school. The black kids didn't want to hang around with her because they felt she wasn't like them. The white kids did not want nothing to do with her because to them she wasn't white. It wasn't nice the way they treated her, calling her stupid names like zebra, vanilla fudge, you know all that stupid shit. She put up with a lot of shit from people. I hadn't seen her in a long time, and sometimes I would wonder what ever became of her. So, needless to say, I was surprised to see her in Reading working as a call girl. From what I understand, at that time she had to fend for herself. I guess she had to make money anyway she could. She was very attractive, and she still is. She got into a situation that the rest of her life she's going have to deal with."

"Okay, Don, you sparked my interest. I'd like to talk to her. Let me ask you some questions: What's this girl's name, do you think she'll talk to me, and how do I go about finding her?"

"Tony, I'm already ahead of you. I talked to her, and I did ask her if she'd be willing to talk to you, maybe give you some information about what she knows about these guys. She said she will do what she can do for you. Like I said, she's always been good to me. Her name is Conjetta Reynolds. I knew her as Connie. I really do not know where she lives now. I do know she doesn't live in North Oak anymore. She lives in Reading somewhere and moved there some time ago. I do know that some of her family was from the town of Green Hill. That's all I really know. I did get a phone number for you. It's the best I can do for right now."

"You did good, Don, and thank you for keeping me in mind. I want you to know that I will treat her with the upmost respect. I can only imagine how hard it must've been for her growing up in this town, having parents from different races. I'm sure you did the best you could trying to help her out in school, and I'm sure the kids she was growing up with could've been brutal and condescending to someone like her. I'll give her a call tomorrow, and I'll try and set a meeting. Thanks again for getting in touch with me. Thanks again, I'll talk to you later."

Lupo was starting to think about the time frame that Connie told Don that the two guys from Italy were in North Oak . He started to contemplate the date of the last murders and the time frame when the two fellows were here. He knew he wanted to talk to Connie to get as much information as he could about the two guys from Italy.

18 Uptight

I t was Wednesday morning, a beautiful, cold sunny day as the fog lift-ed from the day before. It was 9:45 in the morning, and Lupo knew that Connie Reynolds requested to meet in a public place. Now, the only angle he had for her not to back out of this deal was by telling her if she did not come and talk with him voluntarily at the police station, she would be seen as withholding evidence on a murder case and then the police could pick her up. He knew that he did not want to play hard ass with her; because if he did, it may only alienate her from confiding in him. Also, he didn't want to alienate himself from Sergeant Baker. He liked Baker and wanted to be straight up with him all the way. The only other way to convince Connie to speak with him was for her to meet him at the police station, and he would make sure that Sergeant Baker would be there. Lupo knew he had to talk with Chief Ryder and Sergeant Baker to see if they both were in agreement for this meeting to take place. Lupo knew he had to throw the dice and hoped that it would come up seven. He finally made the phone call and spoke with Connie about the meeting. She was okay with a meeting at the police station; she felt comfortable as long as Sergeant Don Baker would be attending. She insisted that the meeting be as discreet as possible.

As Tony was going through some paperwork, Chubbs walked over to his desk and informed him that the chief wanted to see them in his office in a couple of minutes. Lupo acknowledged the information that he got from Chubbs and told him he had to go to the men's room and would meet them up in the chief's office.

When Lupo arrived at the chief's office, Chubbs was sitting in a chair on the front left side of the chief's desk. The chief sitting in his chair behind his desk tapping a pencil on his desk calendar.

"Good morning, Lieutenant, please shut the door."

"Oh, you call me Lieutenant now? It's not Tony anymore? What happened? We're not on a first name basis any more, Emery?"

Chief Ryder gave no response to what Lupo said, he just continued to tap his pencil. Then he stopped tapping for a moment and pointed his pencil in the direction of Sergeant McFadden and said, "I was just starting to tell Detective McFadden here about what's coming down from the top. It seems that the DA and the mayor want to wrap up this case about the evil eye murders once and for all. The perp is in jail. It seems that they believe we're spending too much time, or actually wasting time, on the case when we have a conviction. It also doesn't help what they're reading in the papers and what the press is saying about loansharking and some possible other avenues of money laundering that may be connected. So, to make it real simple… they want this over soon, you know, like yesterday."

"Chief, let me ask you a question, if I may. Do the DA and the mayor know that we possibly have some underworld connections?"

"Yes, they do. I have informed them about these issues myself. Now, listen to me, Detective, I know where you're going to go with this. I think between me, you, and Detective McFadden, I've given you the benefit of the doubt. I believe also that the mayor and the DA have good reason to shut down this investigation, the biggest reason being we have a conviction. Now, I'm not here to give you guys a hard time or to break your balls, I'm just telling you what's coming down from the top, and I'm just doing the best I can."

"Listen, Chief, I just got a lead that I think is a pretty good one. I want to talk to someone that may know something more about this case involving loansharking and corruption. It may be connected in part with the underworld. If we can follow this up, I'm sure it could lead us to another avenue with the murders and possibly could prove that there just may be more than one individual besides the watchmaker's son. You got to understand what I'm talking about. You and I talked about the possibilities of underworld connections right after Mr. and Mrs. Padrona were killed. I distinctly remember you were adamant about the possibility of some mafia connections, and you also said that maybe a hired hand came in to do the dirty work."

"Yes, I remember that, Detective, I got a good memory. I remember all of it, but that was before we had a person who confessed to the murders and was convicted of the crime".

"Hold on for minute, Chief, he did not confess to killing **all the victims** involved in the crime. I remember right after he was captured that everyone and their mother was up in our offices celebrating and congratulating one another like they just won the grand prize. Remember I asked you if I could talked to the suspect and **you** told me to go ahead and just let you know if I need you. Well, I asked him at that time in the interrogation room directly to his face, 'Did you kill the Padrona couple?' And he shouted 'no' to me '**NO**'. I do agree with you, Chief, that he may have killed this one or that one. You and I specifically questioned the theory that maybe he had help and that there could have been a possibility of someone else that either murdrered some of the victims or helped him commit all of the murders."

"Yes, I distinctly remember that, and if my memory serves me correctly, I remember he was talking about killing witches and warlocks and all that kind of bullshit. People coming from Italy, the old country as you call it, to kill these people. Or people who are living right here in our hometown hiding someone who murdered someone back in the old country. Listen to yourself, Detective, it all sounds to me like a bunch of bullshit. So whether this John Volpe guy is crazy, a nut job, goofy, insane, whatever the hell you want to call it, whether he told you he was killing witches or warlocks—whatever the hell it was—the bottom line, Detective, is.…. **he was killing people.**"

"Yes, I understand, but I believe he wasn't the only one. Someone else did it with him or he had help. I want to get the right persons. **We** want to get the right persons. We all want to be right that we finally caught the people connected in the "Evil Eye Murders" and put **their asses in jail**."

"**He's in jail now**, and that's all that the mayor and the DA want to know. **Do you understand? You got it?**"

"Yeah, I got it. I'm not an idiot or some jerk off ass hole, you know."

"Watch your mouth, Detective!"

It was at that time that Chubbs was starting to get concerned that Tony or the chief or possibly both of them we're going to say something that they may both regret. Chubbs already knew that Tony was running off on a tangent trying to make his point, but he just kept on talking. " I don't think that the mayor and the DA understand everything, Chief. Almost everyone in town knows they own legitimate businesses, but we also know that the Padrona family and Nicholas Cattivi were lending money out. Most of the family, if not all of the families, are of Sicilian descent. We talked about how these people would bankroll money to let their familes and friends come in to this country. We worked our balls off on this case."

"Hold on. Listen to me, Detective. You're preaching to the choir. I understand and I get it all: the time and man hours that you men put into this case. But you need to understand that the mayor and some of his people are coming to me about you two guys,especially you, Detective Lupo. It seems that some of these snitches and street thugs that you've been questioning are complaining to some of our other officers and detectives here about being harassed, that they are being pressured. Detective, do you remember that lady, one of your contacts I believe, by the name of Crystal? Well, she's been complaining that she's being harassed by you."

"Harassed by me? That's bullshit. That's what that is."

"Also, remember the guy that you and I were talking about, the one who swears he borrowed money from the Padrona family back in the 50's in order to get his brother's wife's family over here from Italy? Then he said he paid the Padrona family back the money, and he was never pressured again by them?"

"Yeah, Chief, I remember him, and I remember that lady Crystal."

"Well, the guy who borrowed the money has been complaining that you were giving him a hard time, and you put a lot of pressure on him."

"That's bullshit too. Chubbs and I spent hours questioning people to see if anybody knows anything about the case. We were questioning some of our contacts out on the streets. You are the one who suggested for us to get out there and shake some people down. To get some answers today. We questioned some of our snitches, our street buddies, as you call them. We were getting our asses into deep trouble with some people. Do you remember saying to us after the Alfredo couple were killed that you had the press, the politicians, and that the town's people all up your ass? Now, you're telling me and saying to us that the mayor and the DA are satisfied. They want to shut everything down. I've spent days and nights in my office here, not going home until one or two o'clock in the morning. Chubbs and I are out on the streets to all hours of the night, going into the morning hours. When all that the mayor and the D A are doing is just sitting up in their offices jerking off. Now, that we have a conviction, a doubtful one at best, they can come out of their offices to shake hands, pat one another on the back, smile, get their names and pictures in the paper, and we are out here, all of us, breaking our asses to make sure that we did everything the right way, that we got the right guy for all of the murders. I don't want the infamous mayor and the prestigious DA bringing the hammer down on us to make us look like a bad bunch of assholes and to say it was us that screwed up this case, that we did everything wrong. I'm telling you, Chief, I have a good feeling about this lead. I really want to follow up on this one lead. We need to follow up on this."

"**No, Detective, no**. Now you listen to me. That's all you've been doing is talking to different people about this, and that's all it is. It's just another 'I think this' and 'I think that' and 'this is a pretty good lead and maybe a possibility,' and so on and so forth. I've stayed behind you two men as long as I can with this case. Now, I'm getting heat from the top, and **it's my ass that will get burned.**"

"Oh, I see now. I get it. **You're worried about your own ass.**"

It was at that very moment that Chief Ryder slammed his fist down on top of his desk, pushed his chair back, and stood up. Hovering over his desk with both of his hands resting on top of his desk, he shouted directly at Lupo, "**HOLD ON, LIEUTENANT!** Who the hell do you think you're talking to? You better watch your mouth. I'm your boss. I'll bust your ass down to patrolman. You'll be walking the streets of North Oak AGAIN if you keep getting out of line. Am I making myself clear on this matter? Do you understand what I'm saying? Because if you don't, I can make it real hard for you, you got it?"

There was a moment of silence that hovered over the office. It seemed at that very moment a huge vacuum had sucked all the air out of the room. It felt as though voices we're just banging off of walls and spinning around inside with nowhere to go. Whatever was left of any calmness, unity, one for all and all for one was gone. All the feeling of working for justice seemed to dissipate. Anger and the intensity filled the room like air forced into a balloon that is ready to burst.

In the outer rooms of the police station just outside of the chief's office, where other patrolman were working at that time, a silence fell as well, they could hear all of the commotion and were taking notice of the confrontation that was going on inside the chief's office. Some of the officers in the outer room were looking at each other, shaking their heads back-and-forth. They knew it didn't sound good. As they looked at one another, a few officers vocally acknowleded to one another the frustration that was coming from inside the office.

It was at that moment that Sergeant McFadden stood up, raised up his hands, and tried to calm the situation down. "Excuse me, Chief and Lieutenant, hold on for a minute. Can I say something? The other officers in the patrol room are concerned. They can hear what we're talking about. I believe that the whole town of North Oak can hear us. If I may just say something, can we just calm down for minute. Let's take it easy and try to control ourselves. Please Chief, and Tony, just for minute... for one minute, guys?"

Chief Ryder was still standing hovering over his desk. He looked to the side of his office where Sergeant McFadden was standing. He then turned and looked up over where Lieutenant Lupo had been sitting and noticed a few of the patrolmen and officers outside his office we're standing there looking into his office in amazement.

Chief Ryder sat back down in his chair. Rubbing the top of his head with his left hand, he spoke to the two detectives. "Okay.... Okay, you're right, Detective. We need to calm down. We're not going to get anywhere with us yelling at one another."

Detective Lupo sat back down in his chair as he agreed with the police chief's statement. "Listen, Chief....I'm sorry if I got out of line. You're right, you have given Chubbs and me a lot of rope. You have given us a lot of support, and I truly believe that you have our backs. I can say for myself, and I think I can speak for Chubbs, that we don't want to cause you any undue aggravation. I know myself I don't need you or anyone else to tell me I'm getting too involved in this case. Between the three of us, my marriage is on the rocks, and I'm trying to deal with that. So, I apologize to both of you for getting out of line. I am sorry."

Chief Ryder leaned back in this chair, straightened out the knot in his tie, and said,

"Okay, Tony, tell me about the lead that you may have. But I got to be honest with you, this is it. Whatever you get from this lead, is it. End of the road. I'll let you guys take a chance to find out what you can. Report back to me so we can talk about it, but I'm telling you straight up. This is it end of the story, got it? I can't cover your asses anymore. I know you guys are doing the best you can, so follow up on whatever you're doing. I'll give you as much time as I can, and then that's all. I'm telling both of you right now; and I'm as serious as a heart attack, I am not losing my job over this case. I want to put this thing to bed for good."

Lupo then calmly reported to the chief and Chubbs about the meeting he had with Bob Salvi and his Uncle Carlo Vanbessai. He told them again of the possible connections with the underworld, on the loan sharking and money laundering aspects of the case. He also informed them of possible connections to people like Louie Wash and other people that may be connected from Italy. He explained how they smuggled them over from Sicily. He told them that he would like to follow up on a prostitute name Connie Reynolds. Lupo informed them that they may be able to tie the connections of the evil eye murders to possible underworld activity.

Chief Ryder gave the go-ahead for Lupo to investigate Connie Reynolds. He again informed both Lupo and Chubbs that this was the last bit of information he was going to allow into the case. The two men acknowledged that they fully understood the circumstances they were in. As they left the chief's office and we're walking down to their offices, Chubbs leaned over and asked Tony to follow him to the downstairs hallway next to the boiler room.

When the two man arrived down stairs, Chubbs then turned around to Tony and said,

"Listen, Tony, this has got to be right, this is really our last chance. I can't lose this job. I got a wife and kids. Personally, I don't want to get involved in your situation at home, and I'm really sorry things are on a rocky road: but as far as I'm concerned, I got to be honest with you, I can't go down with you on this. The chief wasn't bullshitting us. I had also heard about him getting some heat from the top. I got to ask you something and you got to be right up front with me, man. How good is this lead with this prostitute? I mean does she know what's going on or what? Another thing, Tony... are you fucking around with this chick? Because if you are, I can't get involved with this. This is way over my head. So right now, at this moment I need to know the truth. I need to know exactly where you're coming from."

"Listen to me, Chubbs, we go back a long way, you and I. This is my last lead. It could be our trump card. I don't know this girl, and no I'm not screwing around with her. I wouldn't do that to my wife. I know we're on our last leg with this case, and I know the chief is pissed off. I want to tell you something straight up from me. If I go down on this case, I go down alone and hard. I promise you, my friend, you will not go down with me. I'm a big boy and I can take care of myself. I know I got myself physically and emotionally involved in this case. I'm telling you something from my heart: I'm not going to lose my family over my job. I'm not going to lose one of my best friends who has worked with me all these years and who has had my back covered. I know sometimes I can be a hard-headed dago. I know I got myself strongly involved in this case, and I know that sooner or later I'm going to have to let whatever happens happen, but not because I didn't do my job. I'm going to know in my heart that I did the best I could. You're a good friend, and like I said, you always had my back on everything we've done. But believe me, this has got to be my last attempt, and I have to follow up on it. If it goes nowhere, then I'm done. Now, all I ask from you is that you is to trust me on this. I got some loose ends to tie up, and then I got to meet with this girl. I really need to know, Chubbs, are you and I good on this? Are you okay?"

Detective McFadden walked over to the Coca Cola machine, with his head hung down shaking it back-and-forth. Then he turned around to Detective Lupo, pulled up on his belt buckle, and said, "Yeah, Tony, I'm good with this, and we are okay, you know that. You going to handle this alone or do you want me to be with you? The only reason that I'm asking you is, are you sure this girls is not a set up? I mean, if what you're saying is true about the information you got about this guy Louie Wash and with all this bullshit going around about loan sharking, money laundering, mafia, and underworld corruption, you are dealing with some really bad people. Are you sure you're going to be okay? I mean, Tony, you've been asking around a lot, pushing on a lot of people. Look, you know and I know we haven't made a lot of friends, especially you asking a lot of questions about this case. You've been on it a lot more than I have. You've been laying hard and heavy on a lot of people about the one suspect theory. You know as well as me, Tony, you have pissed some people off. I know it, you know it, and the people you've been talking to all know it. I'm just saying this girl's a prostitute. In her line of work she would not be dealing with very friendly people. Like you said, I just want to make sure. I got your back, so that you can go home tonight to kiss your kids and say good night to your wife."

"You know, Chubbs, this is really what it's all about to me: it's about family and friends." He paused. "I will tell you this: I got this lead from Sergeant Don Baker. Remember when he called you and you gave me his information. Baker told me this girl was straight up. It was just something that he thought I might be interested in. I'm supposed to be meeting her later on tonight. I'll be honest with you, I have thought that this could it be a set up. Is somebody out to get me? I don't know. I do know one thing, that both you and the chief know I'll be at the station. I know you got my back and that's all I need to know for now".

"Tony, I don't know about that. I just got a funny feeling. Listen, you and I, we know Sergeant Baker. We know he's on the up and up, but we don't know this girl with all the bullshit that's been going down between the towns of North Oak and Green Hill. Somebody could even be setting up Baker."

Tony Lupo knew that Chubbs had a good point. He also knew he didn't make a lot of friends asking the people around town, good or bad people, if they knew anything about the murders or about the accused, and he knew he was pushing hard to get more information.

19 More Information

Chief Ryder was not so convinced about not only the meeting in general but also about bringing in Sergeant Don Baker at the questioning of Ms.Reynolds. His reasoning to Detective Lupo about Sergeant Baker was his concern about bringing someone from the vice squad into an interrogation. But through Detective Lupo's persisting that Sergeant Baker was the initial point of contact to Connie Reynolds, he assured the chief that it would make Ms.Reynolds feel more comfortable because of her acquaintance with Sergeant Baker. After much convincing, Chief Ryder conceded to Lupo's request with a final notation warning Lupo that this was the last straw and his last card to play.

Sergeant Baker was on board and was more than happy to be of help to both Connie and Tony. The meeting was set for the late evening hours because Lupo knew the station would be quiet at that time of night; and when he explained the situation to Connie, she was okay with that time of night as well.

Lupo's next call was to his wife to let her know he'd be working late. As he expected, the conversation between them did not go very well. Cathy was not happy that he was spending more time down at the police station. She was well aware that it was about the "Evil Eye Murder Case," and she informed her husband that she was at the end of her rope. She also said that when he got home they needed to talk. Tony responded, "Is everything all right with the kids?" Her response back to him was, "The children are not the issue, everything is not all right with us, Tony. You and I both know that." She said goodbye and hung up the phone.

When Sergeant Baker arrived at Detective Lupo's office, the two men conversed about the best way to make Ms. Reynolds feel comfortable. They both agreed it would be to everyone's benefit to be as comfortable as they all could be. Connie Reynolds placed a call to Detective Lupo and told him that she would be there in about a hour. He looked at his watch and noticed that the time was 8:45. Lupo told Connie that Sergeant Maxwell would be working the front desk. When she arrived at the police station, she should mention to Maxwell that she was there to see Detective Lupo. Sergeant Maxwell will call Lupo, and he will come down and escort her to his office.

It was 9:58 when Lupo received a call from the desk informing him that Connie was downstairs in the lobby. Lupo pushed his chair back from his desk and proceeded to walk down the hallway and down the second floor steps to the first floor to greet Connie. As he walked into the lobby, he turned and thanked Sergeant Maxwell and greeted Connie with his out-stretched right hand to shake hers. She placed her hand in Lupo's, and he laid his left hand gently on the top of her hand and thanked her for giving him her time.

Connie Reynolds was a tall slender Woman, about five foot eight, and very attractive. Her rich dark brown hair lay neatly on her shoulders. Her brown skin was accented very nicely with red lipstick and two gold diamond earrings. She wore black slacks and a white silk blouse topped with a black and gray tweed blazer. She wore a beautiful gold sapphire ring on the third finger of her right hand which was highlighted by dark red nail polish. White pearls around her neck finished off her outfit. She spoke clearly and very softly as she greeted Detective Lupo.

"Ms. Reynolds, may I offer you something to drink... a soda or coffee?"

"Just a cup of coffee... black please."

Lupo poured Connie and himself a cup of black coffee. He turned and gave the cup to her and made light conversation about the weather outside as they proceeded to walk towards the elevator to the second floor.

When they arrived at the second floor, Lupo once again reassured her that he wanted her to feel as comfortable as possible. Sergeant Baker was standing next to Lupo's desk. Connie and he greeted one another with smiles and a hug. Sergeant Baker gently kissed her on the left side of her cheek. "Hello, Connie, it's always nice to see you. You look great. I'd personally like to thank you for taking time out to come down and talk to Detective Lupo. He really does appreciate it."

Lupo, wanting the meeting to be comfortable for everyone, did not want to sit behind his desk, so he pulled all three chairs in a circle so it would seem that everyone would be on equal ground.

"Are you comfortable, Ms.Reynolds? Is there anything else I can get for you?"

"No, Detective, I'm fine. Thanks again for the coffee."

"So, Ms.Reynolds, Don Baker informed me about an incident that you had over several months ago. He enlightened me that it may be of some interest to our department about the interactions you had with an individual or individuals and the possibility of a connection with a murder case we have been working on. Now, what I'd like to hear from you is everything and anything you can tell us. So please tell us what happened."

"Actually, Detective, it was sometime after the last couple was murdered. I don't remember their names, but I remember the case vividly."

"The Alfredos were the last couple murdered."

" At that time I was working in Reading at a club called the Pink Persian Cat. It was the middle of the week, a quiet night as I remember. It was cold, damp, and rainy. I guess it was about nine or nine thirty when two men came in to the club. Sarah, our 'mother lady,' actually is the person who set up what kind of girl she feels is appropriate for whatever the customer requests. In other words, if a customer requested a blond-haired girl, a brunette, someone with black hair, an oriental girl, or a black girl, she accommodates them. She would also mention to each customer the time frame that was allotted to them."

"So, men would go with various types of girls for a limited time frame, if I'm understanding you correctly, Ms. Reynolds?"

"Yes, that is correct. Am I to understand that you are a novice at this kind of thing, Detective?"

Lupo and Sergeant Baker got a little laugh from her reply.

"Yes, Ms.Reynolds, you are correct. I am a married man with a loving family, so I guess you could say in your business I would be the new kid on the block."

"Well, that's very good for you, Detective. See in my line of work, I don't meet gentlemen as honest and forthright as you or my friend Sergeant Baker."

"Thank you, Ms.Reynolds. Now, if you don't mind, can you continue about the two fellows and the night in question please?"

"The way I understood how the story went down between Sarah and the two men was that apparently these two guys were from another country. They were from Europe...Italy to be exact. The one guy specifically mentioned to Sarah that he wanted a black girl. When Sarah informed him that there was not a black girl on that night, he said that he had been there before and that he always had a black girl. Sarah mentioned again that there were no black girls working. Apparently, that was not working out for him. There was some confrontation that went back and forth between Sarah and him. Myself and a couple of the other girls could hear the commotion downstairs. Donnie, a guy who was like a bouncer—we called him the fixer was an ex-pro football player, a big guy that didn't take any bullshit—walked down the steps and addressed the situation. At first it seemed like he was going to have to take on the two guys, but Donnie wasn't only just a big guy, he was smart and he knew how to cool down any type of situation that we may have. After about ten minutes of talking back and forth, I heard him mention my name to Sarah. I could hear them talking about my situation and me being half black. Whatever they worked out, I don't really know. All I know is that I had to deal with the one guy who started all of the commotion. The other guy was trying to calm him down. He was talking to him in Italian and was telling him to relax, to calm down, take it easy, they didn't need trouble, and stuff like that."

"Do you remember what his name was? The man you were with ?"

"Yes, Detective, I remember both of their names. The guy I was with—the guy causing all the trouble—his name was Biaggio and the other guys name was Carmen. The reason that I remember their names is because they called each other by name and were speaking to each other in Italian. They didn't know that my father was black and that my mother was a white Italian lady. A lot of people that I meet, especially in the kind of business I'm in, don't know that I can speak and understand Italian. They're only there for one reason and one reason only."

Detective Lupo looked over at Sergeant Baker, nodded his head, and looked over at Ms.Reynolds. "Ms Reynolds, Sergeant Baker informed me that the last time he talked to you, you told him that one of the fellas mentioned the words 'evil eye'. Can you tell me how that came about, and do you remember which one said that?"

"When I got down to the parlor to meet the guy I was to be with, Donnie and Sarah were there and the two men were still talking in Italian. The guy named Biaggio looked at me and said to the other guy that he liked what he saw. He also said to Carmen, "If this whore is not up to my satisfaction, I will put the malocchio on her." That's when the other guy said to him, "I don't want to hear no more about this evil eye bullshit. Just go up stairs and have her grab your *coglione*. Let's have fun tonight with these *Puttanaios,* so we can get the hell back home. I am tired of this country and fed up with all these people involved with this evil eye shit."

Baker interjected, "Wait a minute, Connie and Tony, what do the Italian words mean that you're saying? I'm obviously not Italian, but I know from the murder case that malocchio means evil eye. But what do the other Italian words mean? I don't understand."

"Let me tell him… okay, Detective?"

"Sure, go right ahead."

"These two guys were no different than any other two guys. *Coglione* means testicles and *puttanaio* means whore. Finally, I had to do the time with the troublemaker; and as far as I know, the other guy went with one of the other girls. When he and I got into the room, everything was strictly business. We didn't talk to each other that much. There were times that I thought about talking to him in Italian, but he was really a pig and I didn't have much time for him. I wanted to do my job and get him the hell out. He did, however, leave me a very generous tip. He then asked me if he came back again if he could see me. He said he was from a small town in Sicily, and he was in North Oak on business, and that he may be back to take care of some more business in North Oak."

"Was that all, Ms.Reynolds? Did he tell you anything else about the type of business that he was doing here, or why he was even in North Oak at the time?"

"No, that's all he said. Quite honestly, I do not want to deal with him anymore. He's history. I am done with him, and as far as I'm concerned, never again."

"Ms. Reynolds, I'd like to thank you for coming in and talking to Sergeant Baker and myself, but I want to ask you something. Why did you wait until now to talk to law-enforcement if you had some idea that this person or these two men somehow would be connected with the 'Evil Eye Murder Case.' Why now? Why didn't you come forth before?"

"To tell you the truth, Detective, I don't know why. I have been following this case in the newspaper because of the evil eye theory and the Italian belief that some people have in this theory, and it happened in my hometown. See, I knew the jeweler, the watchmaker, who was involved in the case. I also knew of the watchmaker's son; although, I did not know him personally. Many years ago the watchmaker made me a beautiful necklace. My late, wonderful grandmother on my mother's side of the family bought me this beautiful necklace from Mr.Volpe, the watchmaker, when I was a child. It was a necklace made of 18 karat gold with sapphire's and a picture of the Blessed Virgin Mary. It was my favorite necklace. My mother's side of the family knew Mr.Volpe and his business. They shopped at his jewelry store in North Oak. My mother, who also was a wonderful and great woman, who I love dearly, bought me this ring at Mr. Volpe's store. I can remember he would have his son, the one that was connected to the murders, sitting next to him behind his jewelry counter. Whenever my mother and I would go into his jewelry shop, Mr. Volpe was very kind and sweet to my mom and me. His son was always very quiet and shy. As I remember, he never spoke at all."

"Connie, let me interrupt for minute, please," Baker said. " I don't understand about your grandmother and her dealings with Mr. Volpe and his jewelry business. I told Detective Lupo that, as I understood it, you and your mother were strictly on your own, that neither family wanted anything to do with you or your mother. I don't understand about your grandmother. I don't mean to bring up the past—it was a long time ago—but I'm confused."

At that moment Connie pulled out a white handkerchief from her purse. Her head was hung down and she started to pat her eyes. Detective Lupo and Sergeant Baker looked at each other and shrugged their shoulders as if they said to one another, 'What the hell just happened?' Detective Lupo stood up from his chair and put his hand on top of Connie's shoulder and asked her if she was okay. She replied to Detective Lupo that she needed a moment, she was sorry, and she would be okay. Both Detective Lupo and Sergeant Baker were wondering if they should continue the questioning. Both men did not want to get her emotionally upset, but they wanted to further proceed with the questioning about the connection between Connie's mother, grandmother, and Mr. Volpe. Lupo found it very interesting that Connie was so well informed, and she remembered little details about the Volpe family and their jewelry business.

"My grandmother was the only one from my mother's side of the family that would have anything to do with my mother and me. When my grandfather and my mother passed on, it was my grandmother who was the only one that I was ever close to. She did whatever she could for me, and that's why I did whatever I could for her. She didn't know the kind of life I led. I never told her. I always made good money, and I always told her I was in the investment business. That's all she needed to know.

Near the end of her life, I took care of her at one of the best nursing homes in the area. I knew how it felt that people didn't want to bother with me. That's why I felt a connection with the jeweler, Mr.Volpe, and his son. The people around town would shun me. They would talk terrible about me and my mother. They had no time for Mr.Volpe's son because he was quiet and shy. He was very strange to some of the people in that town. Really, it's probably just like any town in America. If something extremely different happens to you or your family, then you're considered an outcast to some people. They didn't want to bother with you. You're not their kind. They're scared of you. They're afraid to let you into their circle. It's all bullshit, Detective, and you and I know it's true".

"Ms. Reynolds, I need to ask you something. Could it be that the reason you mentioned to Sergeant Baker that you wanted to talk to me about these two men and the evil eye case was because you may have some kind of a bad feelings or a vendetta against some of the folks from North Oak?"

"No, Detective, I have no animosity towards anyone from this town. I came to you because I know that not all of the people in North Oak are evil people. I know and I understand that there are some good people in this town that are just like you and Sergeant Baker. I also know that some of these people in town would not believe someone in my line of work. To them, I'm the kind of person that deals with very unscrupulous types. In their minds, that's all they can see. To be very honest with you, I could care less about those type of people. That was the very reason that I left North Oak and moved up to Reading. In reality, it was only about a fifty to sixty minute drive from North Oak , but I was in a place where no one knew who I was, where I came from, or what I did. That was what I needed then and quite honestly now. The life I have is the kind of life that I choose. It's like my mother would say to me: 'You made your bed, now lay in it.' I don't what you or anyone to feel sorry for me. I don't feel sorry for myself; this is not a pity party. I don't mean to complicate your investigation any further about the evil eye murders. I simply wanted to let you know that there may be some strange or maybe some very questionable connections between these people and the murder case. That's all I have to say. I have no ulterior motive to harm or hurt anyone else or to add any more confusion to either you or Sergeant Baker. I hope you understand and believe me. There is something maybe I should mention to you at this time: I believe that my time is limited. By that I mean my life here on earth may be limited. I have recently found out that I was diagnosed with pancreatic cancer. The doctors informed me it could be terminal. There is nothing that anyone can do for me."

At that very moment, Detective Lupo sat back down in his chair. He turned his head to the right to look over at Sergeant Baker who was sitting, leaning back in his chair with his two hands lying gently on his thighs with a look of disbelief upon his face. He looked as though he was trying to make some sense of what he had just heard. All the air inside the room seemed to evaporate. There was no sound, just total silence. Both Lupo and Sergeant Baker seemed to be experiencing an overwhelming sensation. Lupo felt as though he was a thousand miles away from the conversation. For the first time, in a long time, he felt a weird out of body experience. He questioned himself if he was truly hearing what he had just heard. In an emotional way he felt her pain, her loneliness, sorrow, and anger. There was a certain type of emptiness inside of him that was confusing and unthinkable also.

"Detective Lupo, are we done now? Have we concluded our meeting? I'm sorry but I am getting tired. I'd like to head back now, if that's okay?"

"Yes...oh yes, Ms.Reynolds, we are done here. I must tell you I'm so sorry. Is there anything that I can do for you?"

"Connie, I'm very sorry to hear about your illness. I don't know what to say. Like Detective Lupo, I'm shocked. I'm very very sorry. Please can we help you anyway?" Sergeant Baker asked.

"No thank you, gentlemen, there is nothing that you or anyone can do right now. I hope what I've told you will help you in some way. I must say I thank you, Don, for the times you were there to support me."

Baker and Detective Lupo escorted Connie to the first floor of the police station and walked her out to her car. Before she entered her car, she shook hands with Detective Lupo and wished him well. She turned around and hugged Don gently, kissed him on the cheek as she thanked him again. As Ms.Reynold's car was pulling away from the police station and driving up Airy Street, the two men stood in the misty rain as they watched the exhaust from her vehicle disappear into the damp night air.

It had been an eventful meeting to say the least. Sergeant Baker sighed and said, "I'm around if you need me for anything." Lupo thanked him for coming. He told him that he would also be in touch with him. He walked over to his desk, jotted down some notes on a piece of paper, laid his number two pencil down, and sat back in his chair, wondering what type of situation would be waiting for him when he arrived at home. He knew from the conversation he had earlier with his wife that she was not happy with their relationship as both husband and family man. Lupo himself knew she was right. He knew he did not want to argue with her about their relationship. He loved his wife, he loved his children, and he loved the life he had with them. He wondered if all this police work was finally getting to him. He knew one thing and only one thing: He did not want to lose his family. He knew that for sure. He was only hoping that when he got home that she would be in bed sleeping. He looked at his watch; the possibility of her being in bed asleep was good because it was 11:20. He had a very long and trying day. He was physically and mentally drained, and he had had about enough conversations that day and night for a hundred years.

20 Last Stand

ony Lupo was correct: his wife was asleep when he arrived home. He was also right that she was not happy with their relationship. At 8:13 a.m. Lupo made his way from his bedroom downstairs. As he walked past the dining room table, there was a note on the table from his wife that said, *I took the kids to school. When I come back home, we need to talk, so please wait for me before you go to work.* He then walked into the kitchen; and as he was standing over the coffee pot and pouring himself a cup of coffee, he heard the front door close shut. He sipped his coffee, looked out of the front kitchen window, and did not turn around. Cathy walked into the kitchen and stood there and confronted her husband. She was precise and to the point about the one thing that Tony Lupo did not want to hear. "I want a divorce."

Tony stood there looking out of the window directing his eyes on the bird that was nesting on a tree branch of the oak tree that he and Cathy had planted in their backyard. Tony's wife said again. "Did you hear me, Tony? I want a divorce."

Tony put his coffee cup down, turned around to his wife, and said, "**I don't want a divorce.** We don't need a divorce. I know that a lot of this and possibly all of this is my fault. I understand now that my police work has gotten too much involved in our life. I understand now fully that I was wrong in my duties as a husband and as a father. I will tell you this from the bottom of my heart. I do not want to lose you. I do not want to lose my children, and I definitely do not want to lose the family life I have." "Well, Tony, I am at the end of my rope. I have really had it. I'm tired. I don't want to continue my life like this, our life like this. You're right about the job.I mean who in the hell would forget their wife's Christmas gift on Christmas day and keep it down at the police station? Who else spends days and even nights sleeping in a chair behind a desk at the police station? Yes, Tony, it's true there have been nights that you don't even come home. And when you do come home in the morning, you give me a kiss, ask me how our kids are, go upstairs, shower and shave, and you're off again. And I'm supposed to feel good about that? I should understand all of that? Well, here's a real surprise for you, Tony. **I don't feel good about what's going on, and I don't understand what's going on.** What I understand is that you spend a hundred and forty nine percent of your time either out on the streets or down at the police station on this murder case, this evil eye case, a murder case that I'm quite sure other detectives can handle. You have good men down there that can do exactly the same thing you're doing and maybe even better.And the other 1% out of the hundred and fifty percent, Tony, is spent on me and the kids. **That's what I really understand."**

Cathy could no longer hold her emotions back. She felt her adrenaline was swiftly encompassing her whole body. She started to feel the tightness in her throat and her eyes fill with tears. She wanted to be strong and not to breakdown. She fully understood that she could not let her Irish temper get the best of her now, and at the same time she didn't want to feel weak, frightened, or lose control of her emotions.

"You know something, Tony, you're being a real son of a bitch about all of this. To be honest with you, I feel sorry for our kids. There's times when they ask me, 'Mom, when is daddy coming home and why is he working all the time?'"

"You're right about everything you said. You are right and I'm wrong. I see that now. It's my fault I didn't see this happening to us and to our children. There are a lot of things about our life at home that I have neglected. I'll tell you now, with all my heart and soul, I truly am sorry. I didn't have a chance to tell you something. Chief Ryder has given Chubbs and me an ultimatum: we have to wrap up any and all investigations that we're doing on this case because he's getting some heat from the mayor and the DA. I don't want to lose my job; but most important, I don't want to lose you and my family. If you can see your way to hang in there with me so that I can talk to the chief; I not only want to save our marriage, but I do not want my friend Chubbs to lose his job. I'm telling you the whole truth. I will talk to him as soon as I can about moving on from here. I ask you, Please give me another chance?"

"I don't know, Tony. I'm tired of worrying day and night if or when you 're going to come home. I'm tired of worring if Anthony, Jennifer, and Michael are going to have a father to watch them grow up, to help them grow up through grade school and high school. I'm really tired of worrying about us. I'm sorry, Tony, I am truly sorry, but we need time away from one another. I need time away."

As he was driving to work, Lupo was contemplating a ton of thoughts that were spinning and spinning around in his mind. He did not have a good feeling about the conversation he had had with Cathy and the way they had left each other. He thought about his children, about the kind of life that they would have if he wasn't around all the time. He thought about his parents, about the ups and downs that they had to deal with in their life. The way they left Italy, came to America with three children, set up the house that is a home, and set up a business that was their livelihood. His father was a strong and intelligent man. Lupo was thinking he'd like to be as strong and intelligent as his father. He thought about the everyday police business that he had to deal with. He thought about the interviews, the people he talked with, and some of the cases he had worked on. He thought about the evil eye murders and if he really was just grabbing at straws. He thought about how good he had it and that his family was healthy. He thought about Ms.Reynolds and the kind of life that she had growing up the way she did, the type of loneliness and the pain that she must have had to deal with every day. He knew he didn't even have anywhere close to that and he was grateful.

When he arrived at the office, he greeted his partner in crime and informed him that they should meet with Chief Ryder and enlighten him about the interview with Connie Reynolds. As they were walking to the office, Lupo and Chubbs made small talk about the interview with Ms Reynolds. As they approached the chief's office, his door was closed and he was talking on the phone. They knocked on the door and the chief waved to them to enter as he was hanging up the phone. Lupo informed both men about the interview with Ms.Reynolds, about what she knows and does not know. He told them what he thought they should do. As far as Lupo was concerned, he wanted to follow up on the lead, but he knew that the final decision was going to be up to his chief. Chief Ryder did not seem to be very impressed with the information that he was receiving from Detective Lupo. The chief informed both men that he thought it was suspicious and that it probably would not hold water in a court of law. He also informed his men that it could be just a big coincidence that the two men from Italy were in the area around the same time of the evil eye murders. It would also be hard to prove, with what they now know from Ms.Reynolds, that the two men from Italy had anything at all to do with the "Evil Eye Murder Case." After about a half hour of talking about the meeting with Ms.Reynolds and going back and forth with questions and answers from both Chief Ryder and Detective McFadden, the chief told them to dig a little further, but he reassured them there was a time limit on this case and he informed them again that they already had spent too much time on it. As the two men were getting up and walking out of the chief's office, he made one more comment to them before they opened his door. "Remember what I said. We have a conviction and everything points to him. I went along with you, and I have given you the benefit of the doubt as much as I could. This is the final straw. Personally, I think you guys are just pissing in the wind."

The two police officers did not turn around as Detective McFadden opened the door and walked out. Detective Lupo started to walk out but grabbed the door knob and turned around to Chief Ryder and said to him. "Thanks for giving us this last chance. I fully understand what you're saying, and you just may be right."

21 The Way It Is

T ime was moving. Minutes were turning into hours, hours were turning into days, days turning into weeks. It was especially a very difficult time for Detective Lupo as the clock just kept on ticking. He knew his days were numbered about his theory of more then one suspect on the evil eye murders. He also was aware that things did not look good with his relationship with his wife and with his family. He wondered what type of life he had now that he was living out of a suitcase at the local Holiday Inn.

His memory was flashing back to the Christmas when he and Cathy were arguing about how much time he was spending down at the police station working on this case. He remembered back to the time he forgot her Christmas gift that he left at the police station. Now, he was thinking she was right: back then his work at the police station on the evil eye case was and still is his life. He only needed to have that type of memory to reassure himself that he didn't want to end up without a family to be with and to love, especially around the holidays. He remembered how happy she was about being pregnant with such a wonderful Christmas gift with the birth of their third child. He now wanted his holidays to be filled with love and joy with his family.

He was tired of working around the clock on holiday weekends. His memory floated back to the first couple murdered, the Padrona family; their murders were just a few days before Thanksgiving. And his memory again brought up the dark side of the murder of Mr. Nicholas Cattivi that took place around the Christmas holiday. In his mind he wanted happiness and love. He didn't want to deal with these unheinous crimes. In his heart and soul he knew it was about faith, love, and family, and he wanted to move in a positive way. His partner in crime, Chubbs Mc-Fadden, was actually getting tired of the murder case. There was a strain not only with their partership but also Lupo's family problems were not helping much either. Tony's wife and Chubbs's wife are very close.

Tony was working day and night almost seven days a week. The way he was thinking was why not work. He could not go home because of their separation. Sitting by himself, he was thinking about a quotation that he had read sometime ago when he was doing an investigation at one of the local nursing homes that said, *"Now I sit quiet and alone, thoughts of past days, and now those days are going when life was young." I have to stop thinking like this because I'm feeling sorry for myself and that is something I'm not going to do.*

So, for the time being the only thing he had to keep himself busy was his police work. His office was his sanctuary. That's where he would talk on the phone to his children to make sure they were being good for their mother and to tell them that he missed them. There were times late in the evening he would investigate what he thought would be possible leads. He would find himself again entering some rough areas with some very unscrupulous people. He spent time in pool halls, gambling joints, bars, and brothels just trying to dig up whatever he could to possibly find, still searching for another suspect in the case. What he was not getting or understanding was that he was pushing too hard. He was told before from Chief Ryder and Detective McFadden and certain other individuals that he should stop all questions about the case. He better take it easy because he was going down a road that no one wants to go down. There were times that he would wonder if he would make it to the next day. He knew some of the areas he was working in were not safe for anyone except the locals who lived in that area. It wasn't a very positive thing for a detective to be wandering around by himself.

There was one evening in particular when he was investigating some individuals he thought would have possible underworld connections. As he was leaving the pool hall, he noticed on the windshield of his car under the driver's side windshield wiper something that looked like a ticket. As he walked up to his car and retrieved it, it was not a ticket, it was a simple piece of paper that read: **Detective, stop what you're doing NOW. It's over. IT IS OVER.** As he was standing along the driver's side of his car, he turned his head and looked from side to side, up and down the street. All he saw in the damp, misty night air was the vapors coming up from the storm drains in the street as they dissipated into the darkness. At this time in his life, Lupo felt like a stranger in his own town. He wondered if this note could be from someone involved in the murders, or possibly maybe a loved one connected to the victims, a loved one that possibly wanted the die to be cast, who simply wanted their loved ones to rest in peace. He looked up at the streetlights that stood along the sidewalks and noticed the glare shining down on the wet road that reflected the building off the wet section that stood along the small grass covered lawns. Then he noticed a phone booth. He knew that he was at the location of the phone booth where he saw the phone dangling when they investigated the murder of Mr. Cattivi over six years ago. It was at that time that he actually thought about the victims themselves. As he stood there, he started to think about the victim's loved ones. He began to think about their children, their brothers and sisters, mothers and fathers. Then he thought about his own family, his wife, his children, his parents. The thoughts were entering into his mind like a top spinning around, flashing images and thoughts for him to contemplate. The thoughts just kept coming and coming, the thoughts of the evil eye investigation. Was it actually over? Was it true about the one suspect theory? Did he really give it his best shot? Did the investigation with the murders conflict with his family life? These were just some of the thoughts that were going around in his mind. He folded the paper in his hand that the note was written on, put it inside his sport coat pocket, got into his car, and drove back to his room at the hotel.

It was a rainy Tuesday morning about 9:25. Both Detective Lupo and Detective McFadden we're sitting at their desks. Chief Ryder walked up to Lupo's desk and said to him that he wanted to see Lupo and McFadden in his office in five minutes. The chief turned around and walked back to his office.

Detective Lupo turned around and looked at McFadden and informed him that the chief wanted to see both of them in his office in five minutes. McFadden acknowledged what Lupo said and informed him he had to go to the men's room, and he would be right back to wait for him, and they would walk up together. As the two men proceeded to walk up the stairs to Chief Ryder's office, there was no conversation at all between them. When they got to the second floor, Lupo knocked on the door and could here a voice respond by saying, "Come on in." As the two men entered the room, Chief Ryder told them to shut the door and have a seat. Chief Ryder was sitting in his chair with his hands folded on top of his desk twirling his two thumbs and said, "I received a call about fifteen minutes ago from the DA's Office. The mayor wants all and any further investigations on the 'Evil Eye Murder Case' to stop immediately, and the DA concurs with the mayor's statement. The DA also informed me about the one lead that you interviewed a few weeks ago, Tony, you know the lady named Connie Reynolds. Well, I am sorry to say...but... she died. The Reading police department found her last night."

"**Dead!** Where and when did this happen?"

"The Reading police found her in her apartment. They found her in the bedroom with an overdose of pills."

"This is hard to believe, Chief. Sergeant Baker and I just interviewed her a few weeks ago and she seemed to be mentally okay. Are they sure about what they found? I mean could there have been any foul play involved? What we found out doing our questioning was that she dealt with maybe some unscrupulous people that may have been involved with the evil eye case."

"I know where you're going with this, Tony. I know that you and Detective McFadden put a lot of time and effort into the case. Especially you, Tony, I know how involved you got. What we know from our counterparts at the Reading Police Department and upon their thorough investigation—I might add that they have some very good people up there—her death was not related to any suspicious activity involving the evil eye case. Furthermore, the two individuals that you and Sergeant

Baker were questioning Connie Reynolds about were out of the country at the time of her death. As for your concern about her death, apparently the coroner's office performed an autopsy and they found out from the autopsy and through further investigation of her medical records that she had cancer. She didn't have long to live. Look, guys, everything is in the report here. Feel free to look it over if you want. I got to tell you this: I've been doing this job for a long time, and I also know, Tony, that you've been on the job for quite some time. I'm sure you understand, now that Connie Reynolds passed away, whatever information you had that we could have presented to the DA is all but gone with her passing. It's a closed case. I don't know what else to say about this. It's coming down from the top, Tony. All I can say to you is I am sorry. It's all over now."

Tony took the report off the chief's desk, and both men walked out of his office. As they walked to their offices, they did not make any conversation to one another. All Tony said to Chubbs was that he was going to look over the report and give it to him when he was done. Chubbs turned to Tony and said, "I don't need to look at it," and walked into his office and closed the door. As Lupo was looking over the report from the Reading Police Department, his interest was centered around what medical information may have added to Miss Reynold's passing. As he was reading the report, the information stated—and it was only a few lines—that no foul play was involved at the time of the investigation. As he read further into the report, he got more involved with the explanation on the medical side of her pancreatic cancer. Reading further into the report, he found out more information about her illness. As he continued to read on about the information that was given on this type of cancer, he was just reading words. His mind was not absorbing what he was reading but only thinking about the life and death of Ms. Reynolds.

For the first time in a long time, the thought of **fire and ice** had reentered his memory. He remembered the same thought of the fire and ice that had entered into his mind over six years ago as he was examining the dead body of Nicolas Cattivi, the third victim of the "Evil Eye Murder Case." Now Lupo was looking at words on a report as if they were a hundred miles away. He was thinking of all five murder victims and about the young lady who took her own life. In reality, they did not want to die. They probably would still like to be living today. He was thinking of Connie Reynolds who took her life at such an early age. He thought about the turmoil in her life, the prejudice from ignorant people she had to deal with. The only sense that he could make out of it was that she possibly didn't want to suffer. She didn't want to lay in a hospital bed sick, lonely, and afraid, just waiting to die. It was possibly the only thing that she could do, and she did it. Then his thoughts went to his own personal life, to his family. He thought of his children: Anthony Junior, his lovely daughter Jennifer, and his little son Michael, then his wonderful and loving wife Cathy. He thought about how hard it must have been for her with the children and what she needed from him to move onward as a family. He poured his whole mind, body, and soul into his police work without possibly understanding the emotions and mental anguish that his wife had to deal with . As all these thoughts were going through his mind, he felt as though he was having an out of body experience. He felt as though his body was sitting at his desk, but his soul was wandering the streets of North Oak, and his mind was slipping away somewhere in a slide zone. All the thoughts just kept coming, and coming again and again. The fire and ice, life and death, love and hate.

"Tony, **TONY, your phone's ringing...** don't you hear it?" Chubbs yelled to him as he was walking over to Tony's desk.

"**Oh yeah,** I got it, Chubbs, thanks. Hello, Detective Lupo, how can I help you?"

"Hello, Tony, it's me Cathy, I'm sorry to bother you at work. Do you think you can stop by the house when you get done work today. The kids are going to stay at my sisters house for a while. I think we need to talk."

"Sure, I can do that. Is everything okay? Did anything happen?"

"No, nothing happened. Everything is okay. We need to talk."

"I will be done here in about forty five minutes, and I'll be right over. Ok?"

"Okay. Tony,...I'll see you then."

Tony was glad to hear from Cathy, but he also had a feeling that he didn't want to hear bad news, the kind of news that had the word divorce in it. Again he had to throw the dice to see if it would roll in his favor. Maybe what they needed was time to just sit down and talk with one another, instead of talking at each other. Tony now knew the difference between the two.

22 Time to Reflect

Detective Lupo called off from work for a couple of days informing the desk sergeant on duty he had some personal business to take care of. On Friday morning when Detective Lupo arrived back at the North Oak Police Department, he parked his car, walked up the stairs of the police station, said good morning to all personnel that were sitting in the outer office. He walked into his office and retrieved a note pad that was in the top left drawer of his desk. He then walked out of his office, closed the door, and knocked on Chief Ryder's door. Chief Ryder was sitting down behind his desk as he waved his hand for Detective Lupo to enter.

"Good morning, Tony, how you doing today? I noticed you took a couple of days off. Are you feeling any better?"

"Yeah, thanks, Chief, I'm feeling a lot better."

"Okay good. What can I help you with?"

"I have this note pad here, Chief, that I have kept over the years. It has all the murder cases that I have worked on since I became a detective, information and notes that I wrote down for myself about the evil eye murders, the Marianne Twitchell murder case in Stoneborough, old murder cases that happened in North Oak, and so on. I just thought that you might be interested in looking through it for yourself."

"Why would I want this, Tony? It's your personal information. We have all our murder reports on file in the cabinets down in the file room. Why would I need your personal notes for me look at? I don't understand; why are you given this to me?"

"One reason, Chief, **I am done. I am out.** I'm going to retire as of right now. I put my time in. I have the years, and I'm going to retire. I'm going to put my papers in today. Out of respect for you and our department, I wanted you to be the first to know. I want to thank you personally for all the support, all the help that you have given me over the years. You have been good to me. I know we have had our ups and downs, but they were very few and far between, and I thank you for that. The time is now, Chief, for me to start a new chapter in my life. I need to move forward and onward. I have a good feeling in my heart and in my mind that I am truly doing the right thing."

"Well...man.... Tony, I got to say this is really a surprise. I am totally shocked. If you don't mind me asking, is it because of your family situation with you and your wife?"

"No, Chief, I don't mind you asking. The answer to that question is no... there is no problem there. Cathy and I sat down and we really talked with one another. We talked about our family, especially our children. Hell, Chief, we talked about a lot. She's with me all the way."

"Okay, Tony, I got to say I personally think everyone here is going to miss you. I know I'm going to miss you. I know you're a damn good detective. You're one hard-working son-of-a-bitch. It sounds like you got all your ducks in row, all your I's dotted and all your T's crossed. All I can say now is for you to go across the street to the courthouse and see Rosalie Carr in personnel. She will draw up all the paperwork you need for your retirement. I wish you good luck, Tony, wherever you're going and whatever you choose to do."

` Chief Ryder and Tony shook hands and hugged one another as they patted each other on the back. Again they wished one another health and goodwill. Tony Lupo took off one month the time off that he had remaining of his vacation time and he received his full police pension and medical benefits for the remainder of his life.

Cathy and Tony sold their house. They moved the family to a place that Cathy and Tony always enjoyed visiting; Lancaster, Pennsylvania. They built a brand new, four bedroom, ranch-style stone home with a full basement, two and a half bathrooms on two and a half acres of land, with a fenced-in backyard so their German Shepherd, Leo, could play in the yard with the kids.Tony started a small locksmith business called.

Tony's Locksmith

(WE WILL ALWAYS OPEN THE DOOR FOR YOU.)

Epilogue Faith, Love, Family, Time

Now that the "Evil Eye Murder Case" has been officially closed, it seemed that some people wanted to voice their opinions about the case. Some people wanted to spread all kinds of rumors. Then there were some people who just loved to gossip. All of a sudden various people in the town who knew about the murder victims, about the murderer himself, and about all the families involved in the evil eye case were talking like they never wanted to talk before.

As the months and years passed, Tony Lupo, who had been retired from the North Oak Police Department for many years, enjoyed sitting on his back deck in the late afternoons talking with his loving wife Cathy and their third dog, also a German Shepherd, named Oscar. Tony had taken a liking to what he always called the police dogs. Leo and Stanley, the two police dogs before Oscar, had passed away from old age. Now, that both Cathy and Tony we're getting into the twilight of their life, they enjoyed sitting on the deck just talking and looking out at the backyard with such a wonderful view of the pristine Lancaster countryside.

As he would sit and look out at his backyard, he would sip smoothly from his glass of homemade wine. Thoughts would enter into his mind like the clouds that fade away into the afternoon sky. Some of the thoughts that entered his mind were of the times and days that have gone by, about some people he worked with in the police department, his old police chief Emery (Frank) Ryder who moved his family to Naples, Florida and passed away five years after he retired from the North Oak police force. Michael (Chubbs) McFadden who retired and is living with his wife in Ocean City, New Jersey; Segerent Don Baker also retired as captain from the North Oak Police Department and is living with his family in Mount Pocono, Pennsylvania.

He thought of John Volpe who spent the remaning years of his life in Outer Ford State prison. Tony started to contemplate what he tried to understand about some people and their family life. At times he would feel a bit of remorse for some of the people he had interviewed while he was working on the murder case. He would think about the young lady,Connie Reynolds, who had to live the life of a prostitute because of the way she was treated in her hometown and by some of her family members. Some thoughts would enter his mind about the man convicted of the crime and his family, for the victims who were murdered and for their families. He thought to himself what a shame for all of the people who were involved, how awful it must've been to go through such a huge and painful ordeal. How much sorrow and heartbreak it took from everyone involved. However, Tony did understand one thing for sure: The family life that he possessed in his own life and his family dating back to his ancestors in Italy were a great deal different from the families involved in the evil eye case.

Lupo started to flashback to his childhood days also thinking about his mother's and father's family and how they enjoyed their family life and all the wonderful stories they would talk about living in Italy. Lupo knew that not only he but his immediate family enjoyed laughing, playing games, playing sports, telling jokes, watching television together, going to the church functions and school yard fun time. He understood and appreciated that growing up with his aunts, uncles, and his cousins was one enjoyable life and time. His mind would begin to wonder about the victims and what their family life was like. He wondered about an individual who would confess to committing such a heinous crime as murder, that he must have had deep concern, not only for his family but for the love he must have had for his mother. No matter how many ways he tried to understand and to make some type of sense out of the case, it always came back to him. That it was... and is always about family.

He did not know why he still was thinking about the people and their families who were involved in the murder case, or what would drive someone over the edge to kill five people in cold blood. John Volpe stated that the victims bothered his family for years and most importantly his mother.

"You want to know something, Cathy, now I know I love my family dearly, but I can honestly say, I truly don't know what I would do if an individual did any harm to any of my family or ended the life of one of my family members. I know to some people this may sound strange: If John Volpe did kill five people, I would like to think he did it not for the money but out of love for his family and most of all his mother. Not that it is right or justified to take anyone's life, it's just that life is so short and in some cases so fragile. Most likely I will never have an answer to that case, and I probably will never know why. Some people will live long and happy lives and some will live with anger and sadness, no matter what or why."

"You know something, Tony, we are truly blessed. You and I have said it over and over, time again, that we have good family values. We tried to teach our children and bring them up the right way, and I think we have accomplished that."

"You're right, we are blessed. We know it and now our children know it. When you stop and think about it...we truly have a good life. For my years on the police force and as a detective, the 'Evil Eye Murder Case' was the most sadistic case I ever had to work on. The years have gone by and everyone involved in the case is old or passed away. If there's anything I have learned from that case is how truly blessed we are and our family is."

In the town of North Oak and the surrounding town of Green Hill many things have changed. Some of the local catholic schools and churches have closed. The local prison in North Oak closed and moved to the town of Hawskville, just 10 miles outside of North Oak. The North Oak Police Department was torn down and made into a parking lot. They constructed a new police station on the corner of Third and Strawberry Streets. The old North Oak Hospital was torn down and remains a vacant grass lot. There is a brand new hospital that is constructed in the town of South Norriton, about four miles on the outskirts of North

Oak. Also a brand-new bridge was constructed above the Schuylkill River connecting the towns of North Oak and Green Hill.

In reality, when it all comes down to it, whoever you talk with from the two towns will say a lot has changed, and some people will say not really that much has changed. In the winter the wind is still cold and the snow will fall. In the summer the days are long and the temperature is hot. Some people will say, "Remember the good old days?" Some people will remember the old North Oak football field where North Oak High School played their home games on a Friday night. The football field is still standing, but the stands are empty. There is the vacant sound of the hometown crowd cheering in the night air. All that is left is the quiet sound of the home team winning with the victory touchdown.

Yes, it's true that there are some very good memories and maybe not so good memories. There are still a lot of good people in any town in America or Italy because it simply is someone's hometown. Whether a person loves his hometown for what it **is,** or an individual wanted to leave his hometown because of what it **was,** the one thing for sure is that one individual chooses to do whatever he or she feels they must do. The peeple in North Oak, Pennsylvania or Caltanissetta, Italy who have remained there or who have moved away from their hometown, may still see the beauty of their memories they had in years gone by. They will still hear the cheering of the football team or their soccer team. They will see themselves playing on the fields. They will hear the voices in their minds from their good and loving parents, their families, their teachers, their priest, and their friends that they have had in their lifetime. They will hear the laughter that they all shared. The people from North Oak who lived there in the 1940s, 1950s, and 1960s will remember a great deal of things that happened, but they'll never forget the good times they shared with one another. They will also hear the echo of laughter from North Oak or Caltanissetta wherever they are. Today, wherever there is a hometown like North Oak, Pennsylvania or Caltanissetta, Italy, one needs to enjoy the town, the people, but most of all they must try to enjoy themselves as much as they can.

Anthony (Tony) Lupo lived to a good old age and ended his life peacefully in the rolling hills of Lancaster, Pennsylvania with his wonderful and loving wife, Cathy, always by his side. All three of their children married and live fun-filled, successful lives. Cathy Lupo spent her remaining older years of her life living with her daughter Jennifer, her son-in-law, and her two beautiful grandchildren until she passed away. Jennifer is a school teacher at a local high school in the town of Lancaster. Michael became a veterinarian who runs his own veterinarian hospital on the outskirts of King of Prussia. As for Anthony Lupo Junior...well he followed in his father's footsteps and became a detective working and living in the town of Wayne, Pennsylvania.

Acknowledgments

I thank God for everything he has given me: my faith, strength, talent and his love.

I thank my mother and father for giving me a great family. I'm greateful for all their love and support .They were always there for my brothers and me. They are truly missed.

Special thanks to my editor Mary Beth Cusack and her husband Jim.

About the author

James T. Vance is a self-published author who has written three novels: *The Malocchio: The EvilEye Murders* (co-authored with a friend), *Mickey Roe,* and *The Watchmaker's Son.* His stories reflect his deep ties to the Italian community, their traditions, and beliefs.

Jim resides with his wife in the Philadelphia suburbs. He loves Italian music, art, food, and spending time with family and friends.

9 781495 831003